RESCUE RIDER

RESCUE RIDER

Janet M. Whyte

James Lorimer & Company Ltd., Publishers
Toronto

James Lorimer & Company Ltd., Publishers acknowledges the support of the Ontario Arts Council. We acknowledge the financial support of the Government of Canada through the Canada Book Fund for our publishing activities. We acknowledge the support of the Canada Council for the Arts which last year invested $20.1 million in writing and publishing throughout Canada. We acknowledge the Government of Ontario through the Ontario Media Development Corporation's Ontario Book Initiative.

Cover Image: iStockphoto

Library and Archives Canada Cataloguing in Publication

Whyte, Janet M.
        Rescue rider / Janet M. Whyte.

(Sports stories)
Issued also in an electronic format.
ISBN 978-1-55277-869-2 (bound).—ISBN 978-1-55277-868-5 (pbk.)

        I. Title. II. Series: Sports stories (Toronto, Ont.)

PS8645.H87R47 2011   jC813'.6   C2011-903902-8

James Lorimer & Company Ltd., Publishers   Distributed in the United States by:
317 Adelaide Street West, Suite 1002   Orca Book Publishers
Toronto, ON, Canada   P.O. Box 468
M5V 1P9   Custer, WA USA
www.lorimer.ca   98240-0468

Printed and bound in Canada
Manufactured by Friesens in Altona, Manitoba, Canada in August, 2011.
Job # 67774

for my Mum
&
for James Sebastian

CONTENTS

PROLOGUE

Nobody knew I was still there.

It was late, dark in South Hill Stables' tack room. I remember I was cleaning my English saddle, polishing until it glowed like honey. As I slung it onto the rack marked "Dev Rani," I felt proud, like that one tiny piece of the world was mine alone.

I heard the big doors of the indoor ring slide open. The stables' owners, Caroline Brennan and Jerry Frederick, were hollering back and forth. I crept into the hallway and plastered myself against a stall door.

Jerry drove his truck, pulling South Hill's horse trailer, right into the indoor ring. Ms. Caroline secured the huge doors, looking right and left like it was all some big secret. Then something started kicking the trailer's gate, and Jerry was yelling like a demon. And then he and Ms. Caroline manhandled this huge creature — this hooded out-of-control horse — into the stable, out of sight.

1 IN THE WINNERS' CIRCLE

Time to show 'em how it's done, Dev thought, carefully arranging the reins in her hands. She pressed with both heels, telling Mirror Glider, South Hill Stables' champion mare, to walk to the gated entrance of the ring. Dev stopped there and remained perched on Mirror Glider's back, waiting for the crew to reset the highest fence.

Dev ran though the course in her mind, picturing each step, every hurdle. While all the other riders had gone straight at the first jump, she planned to use the entire forty-five-second lead time before jumping. No matter how hard it was to give up those seconds, she would run the Glider around the ring, giving the mare a chance to size up the course.

Dev waited for the signal to proceed, then moved into the ring. At the judge's curt nod, she pressed her right boot-heel to Mirror Glider's side, telling the big grey to shift from a trot to a canter. Dev could sense the tension in the crowd as she and Mirror Glider passed the jumps, casually touring the course.

Dev signalled the Glider with both heels and the mare picked up speed. They cleared the first vertical, then flew over a hedge. Next came the water hazard. It was a broad jump, and Mirror Glider had to extend her forelegs as far as she could. Dev stood in the stirrups, leaning forward, keeping low. An eternity of silence passed before Mirror Glider's hooves thumped onto the earth again.

Without missing a beat, Dev urged her horse on. A split second before the next takeoff, Dev bent far forward. Mirror Glider stretched up, up, and over the triple bar. They landed and leaped again; then two more steps, and another leap. Applause erupted as they circled the end of the ring, then doubled back.

Dev wanted to keep the Glider focused. "That's right," she breathed. "Yes, you're a good girl." *And this is a tight corner,* her mind rattled on. *You'll have to change your lead double-quick to make the turn.* At that second, Mirror Glider changed which of her front feet hit the ground first and took off in the other direction.

They floated over the double rail, then approached the "castle," a wide wall of Styrofoam blocks that looked like brick. Dev sat back and Mirror Glider slowed, gathering her hindquarters beneath her. When Dev bent forward, the mare launched herself. Time seemed to slow as the Glider leaped higher and higher. Then Dev moved her hands forward and the big grey threw out her forelegs to clear the hurdle.

They switched back at the end of the ring and flashed over the last few jumps: easy single rails, low, higher, then highest. Now, cantering back to the end of the ring, they could bask in the crowd's enthusiastic applause.

The announcer commended them on a perfect circuit: "That's Dev Rani and Mirror Glider riding for South Hill Stables. Team 33, no faults!"

Dev leaned forward again, patting the Glider's glossy neck as she slowed to a trot. *That was our last round!* Dev thought, trying not to grin. *We made it through the entire competition with only a time fault in the first circuit!*

"This team has been together four years now," the announcer continued. "It's a strong team with the potential to make it all the way to . . ."

Dev had stopped listening. She and the Glider slowed to a dignified walk and moved out of the ring. They joined the lineup at the rail, stopping next to Anna Crawford and her bay jumper, Fire Dancer. Anna was Dev's toughest competitor, her arch-rival. Right now, Anna and Dev were tied.

Dev turned her attention to the next team just as the jumper nicked a rail, bringing it down. Then the jumper missed the water hazard completely, simply running through it, hind legs sliding. Dev stood in her stirrups, holding her breath, as the rider nearly fell.

"Someone's in trouble," Anna whispered smugly.

Dev shrugged, never taking her eyes of the course.

"It's just lucky nobody got hurt."

The team circled and came at the water hazard a second time. Dev knew the jumper was going to shy, and he did, darting to the right with his head tossed high.

The loudspeaker rumbled that the team — a favourite from Burnaby Equestrian — was excused. Looking angry and disappointed, the rider turned her horse and headed out of the ring.

Anna gave Dev a "check this out" look and turned Fire Dancer toward the gate. Dev leaned forward, watching intently as they entered the ring.

At the signal, Anna urged her horse to trot, then canter, heading straight for the first jump. Fire Dancer's forelegs skimmed the rail, then his back legs flicked up to clear it.

An appreciative "ohhh" rippled through the crowd, followed by a burst of applause as Anna took Fire Dancer to the end of the ring, slowing his pace. Dev saw her lean forward and speak to her horse, preparing him for the next jump.

"Crap," Dev muttered. *She learned that from me. Now watch her go ahead and win.*

Anna turned Fire Dancer in the direction of the castle. They sprinted toward it, unexpectedly faking to the left at the very last second.

That's a fault, Dev thought. Then a little voice added sneakily, *And if they do it again, they'll be out of the running completely.*

Anna brought Fire Dancer around the ring again and urged him to speed up right before the jump. The bay hesitated just as he was taking off. He crashed into the castle full on, scattering blocks of fire-engine-red Styrofoam everywhere. For a second, it looked like Fire Dancer might stumble, and a concerned "awww" rippled though the bleachers.

Dev was not sorry to see a look of irritation cross Anna's face. *Too bad,* she said to herself, trying to work up a little sympathy.

Fire Dancer recovered, taking the next jump in an easy stride, and finished. Anna sat back, talking to Fire Dancer soothingly as they trotted out of the ring.

"Team 28, Anna Crawford and Fire Dancer from South Hill Stables," the announcer blared, "with eight faults. Eight faults for Team 28."

Dev patted Mirror Glider's muscular neck as her mind zipped through Team 28's last circuit. There was a lot of strategy to show jumping. Even though it was a set course, each rider had to figure out the best way to approach it. It was all about finding the distance. Was your horse quick off the mark, able to put on a burst of speed at a moment's notice, or did he need a longer run at it, like Fire Dancer? The way Dev saw it, Team 28's mistakes weren't the horse's fault. They were Anna's.

It didn't take the judge long to make his decision. He finished making his notes and handed his clipboard to the announcer.

The announcer's voice cut through the noise from the crowd. "Would teams 42, 16, 28, and 33 please return the ring." In the requested order, the horses and riders filed into the ring and trotted neatly along the rail.

"That's the way we want them," the announcer said. "Fourth place: 42. Third place: 16. Second place: 28. First place: 33!"

The contestants lined up their jumpers in the middle of the ring. The judge went along the row, congratulating each rider and presenting each ribbon. Then the other three teams trotted out, leaving only Dev and Mirror Glider in the ring.

The judge walked to the booth and returned holding a trophy and a huge blue rosette. "From South Hill Stables," the announcer said, "we present today's champion — the one, the only, Team 33 — Dev Rani and Mirror Glider!"

The applause was so wild, Dev could barely hear the judge's next words. "Well done," he said, shaking her hand. "You've got a heck of a career ahead of you."

"I appreciate that, sir," she said, nodding. "Thank you so much!" She held up the cup and blue ribbon triumphantly, finally allowing herself to smile at the spectators. Then she hooked the rosette over her pinkie finger and, nodding graciously to the cheering crowd, carried the trophy out of the ring.

Ms. Caroline, Mirror Glider's owner, met them at the gate. She was decked out in her best show finery:

jodhpurs and boots, black hunt jacket, blond hair twisted up in a fancy French braid. The only thing out of place was her ruffled pink blouse. And maybe her freshly polished fingernails, so bright they were probably visible from space. Dev handed her the trophy.

"This will look good in the case," Ms. Caroline said proudly. She inspected the trophy, which was a horse jumping a fence, from every angle.

Dev swung out of the saddle. Her boots hit the ground for the first time in hours. "And on the website?" she asked.

Ms. Caroline rolled her eyes. "Electronic this and web that. You kids need to open a book once in a while."

"I know, I know," Dev said with a laugh. She mimicked Ms. Caroline's rule: "'Riders must keep a B average to ride in competitions.'"

"Yes, you must," Ms. Caroline said firmly.

Dev led the Glider to South Hill's horse trailer and took off her tack. Then she buffed the grey's shining coat and buckled on her stable blanket. Finally she backed Mirror Glider into the horse trailer next to Frodo, Jenn Monroe's thoroughbred, and swung the door shut.

Jenn Monroe was one of Ms. Caroline's riding students who boarded her horse at South Hill. She was also in a bunch of Dev's classes at school. Dev shook her head. It was weird that, even though they saw each other nearly every day, they actually didn't know each other very well.

Jenn and Ms. Caroline were in the cab of the truck, talking about Jenn's lessons and the techniques she hoped to learn.

"Hey," Dev said, climbing in beside Jenn.

"Congratulations!" Jenn exclaimed, moving over. "That was such a hard course. Frodo and I didn't even make it past the first round!"

"Yeah, it was, and thanks," Dev answered with a quick smile, "but Mirror Glider did most of the work."

"Don't sell yourself short," Ms. Caroline warned. She waved to the driver of the Crawfords' truck, which pulled Fire Dancer's private trailer, to go ahead. Then she started the engine. The Crawford trailer drove past them, all gleaming chrome and shimmering painted flames.

When the two trailers reached South Hill, the stablehand opened the gate, then loped after them. Dev tilted her head to catch Elijah's reflection in the side mirror. With his athletic style and shaggy black hair splayed everywhere, her friend Elijah George looked a lot like the stocky quarterhorse he rode. "So?" he asked as the truck cruised to a stop.

Dev held out the ribbon as she jumped down, smiling broadly.

"Way to go!" Elijah shouted. "I knew you would —"

Anna appeared beside them, all business. "Excuse me," she said pointedly. "I believe there are show horses to take care of?" She smirked like she was joking, but her grey eyes were hard.

"No problem," Elijah said calmly, though his face darkened a bit. "I'll take care of the Glider, too, Dev." He walked quickly to the door of Anna's trailer and unlatched it.

Anna followed him.

Dev glanced at Jenn, who was staring at the ground, her reddish hair curling over her eyes. Dev grabbed Jenn's saddle along with her own and stomped to the tack room. *Why am I even riding in competitions?* she thought. *I'm just a stablehand who trades stall cleaning for riding. So is Elijah. We're not like the others.*

The ones with their own horses, like Anna and Jenn.

She went into the bathroom, slamming the door behind her, and yanked off her hunt jacket, breeches, and boots, the formal getup she wore for every competition. She pulled the bobby pins out of her thick brown hair and let it flop past her shoulders. Then she scrubbed her hands and face, wiping gold-brown shadow away from her green eyes. Her anger faded, too. Things just were what they were. By the time she looked in the mirror, she was her plain old self again.

"Dev!" Ms. Caroline called. "Your father's here to pick you up. I heard him honk the horn. Tell him he's not supposed to do that!"

"Because it scares the horses, I know," Dev muttered. "I'll tell him!" she yelled back. She scooped up the blue ribbon and ran for the door with her jacket, breeches, and boots crammed under her arm. She jumped into her family's van, and her father drove off before she even had her seat belt fastened.

"I don't have time for this," her dad explained distractedly. "Sorry, but there are problems at the restaurant tonight so I have to get right back."

"I know, Dad," Dev said, "but I can't exactly carry my riding clothes on a bike." She smoothed out the jacket, hiding the ribbon beneath it. "Don't you want to know how it went?"

"You won, right?"

"What gave it away?" Dev asked. "You saw the ribbon, didn't you?"

Her dad laughed. "It's not hard to guess. You always win!"

"Not always," Dev said. Definitely not always.

When they got home, her dad rushed back to the restaurant while Dev trudged to their upstairs apartment. Her brother, Ali, was hunched over his laptop, deep into his latest obsession: StarCraft. He looked up absently and pushed his glasses up the bridge of his nose. "Hey! Did you win?"

"It's not about whether you win or lose . . ." Dev trailed the ribbon teasingly. *It's about flying,* she thought, *and the crowd's cheers. It's about cantering around the ring in that final victory lap.*

2 I H8 MONDAYS

Dev banged the off button on her alarm and pulled the covers over her head. Why did Monday morning have to come so early?

"Dev," her father called from the doorway, "you're going to help me close tonight, yes?"

Dev groaned. "Yeah, Dad. I'll be at the restaurant at six."

"Thanks. Now come and eat something."

"I'm not hungry, Dad . . . Dad!" But her father was already gone.

She showered and changed, then shrugged on her jacket as she crammed her feet into her red Converse sneakers.

"Hey! At least take your lunch," her father said as Dev came through the kitchen.

Dev grabbed one of the brown paper bags lined up on the counter and shoved it into her backpack.

"Thanks, Dad. See you tonight! Bye, Ali." Dev waved as she headed down the stairs.

Living over the family restaurant had some advantages. Her dad and uncle were always nearby, there was ready access to fantastic food, and she could keep her stuff in the huge ground-floor storage room.

The downside? There were always trillions of people around — kitchen staff, cooks, waiters and waitresses ("waitroids," Ali called them) — all the people it took to feed half of Vancouver every day. At least, it felt like half. The business-lunch crowd, family dinner swarms, office party gangs . . .

The other downside? Everything tended to smell like coconut.

Dev slung on her backpack, buckled her helmet, and grabbed her bike.

"Congratulations on winning the show yesterday," her uncle San said, peeking around the corner. "Your dad told me about it."

"Thanks," Dev said as she pushed her bike out the door. A little voice in her head added sulkily, *Sure would be nice if Dad said something to me, but I guess that's too much to ask.* She turned to look at her uncle. There was that goofy grin he always wore when she won. *Good old San,* she thought, *always there for me. For all of us.*

"It means a lot, that you notice," Dev said quietly. "If it weren't for you, I wouldn't even be riding, much less competition jumping. I don't think Dad cares."

"Your father is very proud of you —" San smiled, crinkling up his eyes "— and so am I. Now get out of here or you'll be late!"

"Okay, okay!" Dev laughed.

Manu was waiting outside, pretending to rev his bike like a motorcycle.

Dev grinned at him, shaking her head. Sometimes Manu still acted like the pudgy kid she'd met in grade two. He had a round open face, a face you could trust. His unruly jet-black hair stuck straight up in front.

Dev's mind zipped back to her seven-year-old self sitting alone on a swing, crying, grieving her mom's death. Manu hadn't said a word. He'd just plopped down on the swing next to her and waited. He stayed with her and never left.

"Move it, Rani," he mock-snarled.

"Good morning to you, too, and thank you very much," Dev said in a fake Malayalee accent.

"Bye, Devlin," Dad called from the balcony, but the way he pronounced her name kind of sounded like "devil."

Dev tried not to laugh. "It's Dev-lin, Dad," she called back. *"Dev-lin."*

"Bye, Mr. Rani," Manu yelled.

Dev waved and took off up 49th Avenue.

"I'll never get over the crazy names in your family," Manu panted, pulling alongside her.

"Well, first off, look who's talking," Dev shot back as they turned down Fraser Street. "Anyway, my mom was Irish and Brazilian. That's why she called me Devlin and my brother Alejandro — Ali for short."

"She liked to keep 'em guessing?"

"I suppose."

"Dev, I'm sorry. I shouldn't have brought up —"

"It was a long time ago, Manu," Dev said just as they reached the school. She pulled her bike into its regular slot at the end of the long rack. "I don't think much about my mom anymore. Anyway, I like it with just Dad and Ali and Uncle San. You know . . . the guys."

Manu started humming the theme from *Two and a Half Men* until Dev scuffed him on the back of the head.

"See you later?" Manu said.

"Usual spot," Dev confirmed. She had to boot it to her first class.

★★★

Dev had been worried that she was failing science. She became sure of it when her teacher plopped her test results down in front of her. Mr. Davies was too nice to write a huge *F* on it, the way they do in cartoons, but the red *45/100* said it all. Further down the paper, she saw his tiny scrawl: "Dev, you can do better! I won't send a letter home this time, but I need to see improvement. Let me know if you want extra help."

Dev bonked her head on her desk a couple of times. During the next class, social studies, the teacher assigned a local-history project that could be completed individually or in groups. Dev felt a tap on her shoulder.

"Do you want to work with us?" Jenn whispered. "Heather and Carrie and me?"

Dev's mind went blank. She saw Jenn, Heather, and Carrie every day — at school and at South Hill — but they seemed like aliens to her. They came from a different, richer, world. "Uhhh . . ." she said.

"That's okay," Jenn said, waving her hand. "I know you like to work alone."

"It's just that I don't really have time . . ."

"I know," Jenn agreed. "Working in groups takes forever. You spend half the time deciding when and where to meet. I'm stuck with them, but —" she dropped her voice theatrically "— save yourself!"

Dev burst out laughing. "Thanks, anyway, for the invitation."

At the bell, Dev gave Jenn a smile and dashed out of the classroom. She ran up the stairs two at a time until she got to her usual place on the landing. Manu wasn't there. Dev texted him but he didn't answer. Probably forgot to tell her that he had Yearbook Committee or Environment Club or something. She would never understand why Manu had to be such a joiner.

As she wolfed down her lunch, a vegetarian wrap that was her father's specialty, Dev replayed Jenn's words: "I'm stuck with them — save yourself!"

Maybe she wants to be friends. But I don't get it. When Anna was ordering around Elijah and me, Jenn just stood there. She didn't say a thing!

Dev had to admit it was pretty hard to stand up to Anna Crawford. Still, the look on Elijah's face stayed with her. He was usually so sure of himself. He knew everything there was to know about horses and Western riding. But when Anna treated him like nothing, he looked crushed.

Dev pictured her two best friends: Manu, artistic and funny, who was like a walking egg; Elijah, strong and fast, who always knew what to do. She hated that either of them could be hurt by someone like Anna Crawford.

The afternoon was a breeze. Archery in PE, then English, her only class with Manu.

"Where were you?" Dev hissed.

"Sorry," Manu whispered. "I forgot I had GSA."

"Eh?"

"Gay-Straight Alliance."

"Oh really? Since when are you ...? I mean, are you?"

"It's the Gay-*Straight* Alliance," Manu said pointedly.

"Ready to proceed?" Ms. Webster asked, giving them a look.

Manu gave the teacher a thumbs-up, grinning shamelessly as everybody laughed.

At the end of class, Dev crammed her binder into her backpack. "I gotta roll."

"Okay, see you tomorrow," Manu said. "I've got to go take yearbook photos of football players and cheerleaders. Sad face, please."

Dev pretended to weep. "Your life is just so harsh."

By the time she'd shut her locker, Dev had about fifteen minutes before she was due at South Hill.

★★★

Dev grabbed her bike and zipped down 41st Avenue to Granville. Then she coasted all the way to the bottom of the hill and pedalled furiously along the river road to the stables. She went into the tack room, kicked off her shoes, and pulled coveralls over her clothes. She yanked on her rubber boots and grabbed a shovel.

There were ten horses at South Hill — four that Ms. Caroline owned and six boarders. Dev and Elijah cleaned the stalls and groomed the horses every weekday. The boarders' owners were supposed to take care of their horses on the weekends, although most of them paid extra to get out of it.

As they were clearing out the horses' stalls, Elijah leaned on his pitchfork. "You're not as happy as you should be. Spill."

"I'm flunking science," Dev said, amazed at how easily truth came out.

"Is that all?" Elijah spread a forkful of straw around the stall floor.

"Isn't that enough? You know how Ms. Caroline is."

"Did your teacher say 'See me after class' or anything like that?"

"No."

"Is he going to tell your dad?"

"I don't think so."

"Then don't worry about it." Elijah shrugged. "It sounds to me like you're in the clear."

"For now, I guess . . ." Dev dug her shovel into a pile of manure, flipping the whole mess into the wheelbarrow with a practiced toss.

Once the stalls were clean, Dev and Elijah gave each horse a generous flake of timothy hay and brushed them all down. Dev brushed Mirror Glider until she shone. Ms. Caroline always let her horses rest after a show, so Dev had no plans to take the Glider out that day. She went into the tack room and oiled her bridle and saddle, as she always did before and after each show.

Finally she washed up, scrubbing her hands with the stiff brush she kept at the stable for that purpose. After all, it wouldn't do to go home with filthy fingernails, she thought. Dad and Uncle San would probably both barf, or worse, maybe call up Ms. Caroline and scream at her in Malayalam. This last thought made Dev smile as she stripped off her coveralls, hung them on a hook, and squirmed her feet into her runners.

"I've got to get going — dishwashing duty calls," she shouted to Elijah.

"Same time tomorrow," Elijah shouted back.

Dev zoomed up Marine Drive, then puffed up Main. She stashed her bike in the storeroom and ran upstairs to hop into the shower and change. Then she bolted back down to the restaurant kitchen.

"Here," Dad said, "have this before you start."

Dev sat at the back counter and put away a pancake-shaped *masala dosa* smothered in coconut chutney, just the way she liked it. Then she put on her white restaurant apron and got to work.

For the next couple of hours, Dev rinsed cups and plates, then plopped them on the dishwasher conveyer, lost in a rhythmic swish of suds. When all the dishes were finally done and put away, she hung up her apron wearily.

"Tired, Dev?" Dad asked sympathetically.

"A little." Dev smiled. "Why are Mondays so brutal?"

"People gotta eat," her dad and uncle chimed simultaneously.

"See?" Dev said. "That's how you two know you've been married too long."

San swatted at her with a towel but Dev leaped away.

Dad laughed. "Get out of here, you cheeky kid."

"Gladly!" Dev turned and trudged upstairs to her room. She got undressed quietly, because she didn't want to wake her brother, who was softly snoring in his room across the hall. She flopped onto her bed and slept.

3 BROKEN MIRROR

"Would the following riders please step forward," the announcer boomed. "Numbers 14, 28, 33, and 99."

Dev and Mirror Glider were in the Thunderbird Fall Exhibition — the biggest annual show-jumping competition in British Columbia's lower mainland — and the final round was coming up. Dev signalled the Glider to step forward.

"We would like to thank our other contestants," the announcer continued. "They are excused."

The rejected riders left the ring, leaving four finalists.

Dev patted Mirror Glider's neck encouragingly. At Thunderbird, they were expected to stand at attention outside the ring. Dev and the Glider would go third; the wait was going to drive her crazy.

As she watched Team 14 move smoothly through the jumps, Dev calculated where she and Mirror Glider could make up time. A smarter transition at the end of the ring, she thought, and they'd need to take the triple fence faster. A lot faster.

Then Anna and Fire Dancer were on the course. Their circuit was perfect until they reached Fire Dancer's nemesis, the castle jump. They crashed through it, but bravely continued, finally reaching the end and taking their place beside Dev and Mirror Glider.

Dev was totally focused. She moved the Glider into position, impatiently watching the crew repair the castle. Dev couldn't hear anything but her own heartbeat.

The judge gave the signal to proceed. Dev tightened the reins as Mirror Glider leaped onto the course. It was a familiar configuration and they rounded the jumps smoothly: double rails, castle, water hazard. At the end of the ring, Dev urged Mirror Glider to change her lead and surge toward the triple fences.

This was their moment. Where all the other riders had doubled back, giving their horses almost the full length of the ring to run at the three hurdles, Dev and the Glider were going to take them straight on. The Glider just needed to gather her strength in her hindquarters, to focus on height instead of speed. "C'mon, girl," Dev breathed. "You can do this."

The Glider threw out her foreleg awkwardly, trying to lead with the other foot. The big mare seemed to know she needed to pick up the pace, but there wasn't enough time.

As Dev prepared to lean forward, Mirror Glider leaped a fraction too soon. Dev felt her jumper's hind legs catch the rail, and the hurdle's top pole fell behind them. The Glider recovered, taking the second fence smoothly. But the third jump surprised the horse, came too fast. She crashed into it with both front feet.

As the rails bounced to the ground, Mirror Glider landed with a snort, coming to a full stop. There was no point going on. Dev leaned down to peer at the mare's front hooves. Then she swung to the ground.

One of Mirror Glider's shoes was hanging by a nail.

"What a shame," the announcer said sympathetically. "Let's hear it for Team 33, South Hill Stables' Dev Rani and Mirror Glider."

Dev smiled ruefully to herself and waved to the applauding crowd as she and the Glider limped off the course.

A veterinarian met them at the entrance to the ring. She lifted Mirror Glider's foot and examined it, muttering, "Ooh, that's bad." The vet pulled pliers from her back pocket and removed the last nail. Then she handed the shoe to Dev.

"Your horse will be fine, but she'll need to rest that foot awhile," the vet said. "You should have a ferrier file down her hoof, but don't shoe her again for a couple of weeks."

"Okay," Dev said. "I'm just relieved she's all right."

The vet patted the Glider's silver neck. "Bummer. You guys were headed toward the blue ribbon for sure."

"Thank you," Dev said. She turned and led the Glider back to South Hill's waiting horse trailer.

"Next time, don't do that," she chided the horse jokingly. But deep down she knew it was her fault; she had rushed the Glider and thrown her off her stride.

Dev took off Mirror Glider's saddle and buckled on her blanket. Then she loaded the big grey into the trailer, which had the South Hill Stables logo proudly painted on the side. She carefully placed the saddle in the back of the pickup truck. Then she walked slowly to the cab, wishing it would take forever.

Jerry Frederick, the co-owner of South Hill Stables, was waiting in the truck. "You okay?" he asked.

"For now," Dev sighed. "But after we get back to the ranch, I'm pretty sure I'll be dead."

"Oh, come on. Ms. Caroline's not that bad. She'll probably want to talk to you, though."

"Smooth the way for me, will you?"

Jerry shook his trusty cell phone, smiling. "I already did."

★★★

Back at South Hill, Ms. Caroline opened the front gate for them and waited as Dev got down from the truck.

"Jerry called and told me what happened," Ms. Caroline said. "I'm not mad at you. I just want to talk to you. Come with me. Jerry will take care of the Glider."

Dev followed Ms. Caroline into the office, feeling like a sword was dangling over her head. "I'm so sorry,"

Dev began. "It was totally my fault."

"Look, kiddo, stuff happens," Ms. Caroline said. "The important thing is that you're both okay. But I've been meaning to talk to you for a while now."

Ms. Caroline leaned against the edge of her desk. "Dev, we all love Mirror Glider. She's the best jumper I've ever had. But she's fifteen. She's too old for this game."

Dev wanted to say something but couldn't find the words.

"Let's take a little walk." Ms. Caroline put her arm around Dev's shoulders and steered her out of the office. "I've been thinking about this a lot, and I believe you've got a great future ahead of you. But you need the right horse. Going for a spot on Jump Canada's squad is a big commitment and you need a jumper that can go the distance."

Dev nodded. "Uh-huh," was all she said.

They stopped at the far end of the stable. Dev hadn't thought about the horse in this stall since she'd witnessed his mysterious arrival. Ms. Caroline took a carrot out of her pocket and held it flat on her palm. She put her hand through the rails carefully, calling softly. Slowly, gently, a horse's lips brushed her hand and the carrot was gone. Then so was the horse — back into the shadows with his hindquarters to them.

"I want you to work with Zim," Ms. Caroline said to Dev. She pronounced the horse's name with a soft *s* so it sounded like "Sim."

As far as Dev was concerned, it didn't make him any more attractive.

"What do you think?" Ms. Caroline continued. "He's truly an incredible horse and —"

"You have got to be kidding!" Dev burst out. She pictured Zim's arrival — being shoved into the stable, kicking and snorting, out of control.

"He's a fabulous animal," Ms. Caroline insisted. "Somebody just needs to make a commitment to him."

"Who'll organize the wedding?" Dev sassed back.

"I don't know if you've noticed, but show jumping is a team sport," Ms. Caroline said sternly. "You got lucky with Mirror Glider. She taught *you* to be a jumper. Now it's time to return the favour."

Dev let it all sink in for a moment. "And train Zim?"

"Yes. And train Zim."

"This is all coming at me kind of fast," Dev said. "Can I at least sleep on it?"

"Of course," Ms. Caroline said. "In fact, I want you to think this over carefully. The last thing this horse needs is to have somebody run out on him. He's already been abandoned once."

"And why was he abandoned?" Dev challenged. "Maybe he's a bad horse!"

"I don't believe a horse can be bad, just badly trained. They're herd animals and it's up to us to teach them how to behave."

Dev glared down at her gleaming riding boots.

"Zim's past isn't as important as his future. He needs someone to be patient with him."

Dev nodded. The words "Zim's past" echoed in her mind. *If I decide to work with him, I'll need to find out why he's so scared, and what I can do to help him.*

"There's something else," Ms. Caroline said finally. "My brother just bought a farm on Vancouver Island. It's beautiful, lots of open pastures." She reached out and touched Dev's arm. "What I'm trying to say is, I asked my brother to take the Glider, and he agreed. It's time for her to retire."

4 UP IN THE AIR

The lights in Dev's room flicked on and off half a dozen times. Ali stood in the doorway, grinning. "Time for breakfast," he said.

Dev threw a pillow at him.

"Dad says you're supposed to get up," Ali insisted. "He wants to have a family meeting or something."

"Okay, okay. Just give me a second, will ya?"

Ali consulted his watch. "It's been a second."

"Shut the door!" Dev snapped.

Ali shut it in a hurry.

It was hard getting out of bed. Dev didn't remember ever feeling so tired. Her interim report card with its fabulous science mark (Incomplete) and effort score (Unsatisfactory) sat like a gremlin on her dresser. It was just lucky she'd grabbed it out of the mailbox before Dad found it. Otherwise, there would have been what her father liked to call "consequences."

Dev stared at the blue and red rosettes arrayed around her mirror, thinking, *Well, that's the end of that.*

No more blue ribbons for you. No more Mirror Glider. Maybe no more show jumping. She headed into the bathroom to wash up, then quickly yanked her hair into a ponytail.

When she walked into the kitchen, Dad, Uncle San, and Ali were sitting around the table, looking like nesting dolls, perfectly alike except that Ali was smaller and younger. They were all dark, with wavy black hair. They all wore black-framed glasses, the kind that you usually find on scientists in a chemistry lab. Dad and San had thick moustaches that, Ali liked to joke, they'd been born with.

Dev slid onto an empty chair. "Your uncle has something he wants to tell you," Dad said to both his children.

Uncle San's face went red. "Well, it's a happy thing," he began. "Very, very happy!"

O-kay, Dev thought.

"I'm just . . . oh, I don't know what to say!" Uncle San looked at Dad helplessly.

Dad leaned over and patted his younger brother on the shoulder before announcing, "Santhosh is getting married!"

Dev was stunned for a second, then recovered enough to say, "That's great, Uncle San! Congratulations!"

"Does this mean you're moving out?" Ali asked, clearly not happy with the prospect.

"No, no," Dad said. "San and his bride will live here."

Dev didn't like the sound of that. "With us?"

"Well, I guess we could move," Dad joked. "Of course, with us."

A jumble of memories sped through Dev's mind: Uncle San arriving from India after Mom died; San getting her and Ali ready for school; the zillions of times he'd dropped them off and picked them up . . .

San had been the one to take Dev to South Hill the very first time to see if Ms. Caroline would trade riding lessons for stall-cleaning. San had taken Ali to his Capoeira lessons so the Brazilian martial art could remind Ali of their mother. San had come to every single parent-teacher conference. In fact, he had done everything for them. Dev realized, with a pang almost like fear, that she and Ali weren't going to have him to themselves anymore.

And everything would change.

Dad and San and Ali were all talking and laughing, eating little doughnut-shaped *vada* and drinking iced tea like everything was perfect. Dev couldn't understand why Ali wasn't upset.

Don't you get it? she thought. *He's going to bring some woman in here whose makeup and girlie crap will take up all the shelves in the bathroom. She'll probably nag us to clean our rooms and put up awful pictures of sunsets and babies dressed as flowers.*

Dad was looking at her curiously. "Why are you so quiet?" he asked.

"Well, I kind of have an announcement, too," Dev said.

"Is everything all right?" San asked.

"Yeah, everything's fine. Except that I'm probably finished as a rider. Not that anyone cares." Dev didn't like the bitter tone in her voice, but she couldn't help it.

"I care," San began, but Dad talked over him.

"That's probably good because we're going to need you here," he said. "I was hoping you could learn to do some cooking."

San gave him a look.

"What?" Dad said. "You're going to India for your honeymoon, so I thought maybe . . ."

"Maybe this is not a good time to talk about it," San said gently. He turned to Dev. "What happened?"

"Mirror Glider got hurt," Dev whispered, "and now Ms. Caroline wants her to go live on a farm."

"That's a shame." San looked sympathetic.

Ali looked troubled. "Is that a cute way of saying Mirror Glider's going to die?"

"No," Dev said, smiling a little. "It's called 'putting her out to pasture.' She's actually going to live on a farm."

"But you were doing so well," Dad said finally. "There's no other horse you could ride?"

"Ms. Caroline uses Shelby and Rosie for lessons, and Jack's just a dumb old Western horse —" Dev made a mental note to apologize to Jack the next time she saw him "— and anyway, Elijah rides him. So that just leaves Zim."

"What's Zim?" Dad asked.

"This crazy horse Ms. Caroline wants me to train. She got him a few weeks ago. She said he's a pure-bred Arabian. But he's big for an Arabian, almost sixteen hands tall. His head is beautiful, though, delicate like a deer's and . . ." Dev realized they were staring at her. "What?"

"I can tell you don't like this horse at all," San said.

Dev ignored his sarcasm and continued, "There's only one problem — no one can get near him. I think something's really wrong with him."

"How can Ms. Caroline afford to keep a horse no-body can ride?" Dad asked.

"She can't," Dev said, then realized it was true. She'd have to get rid of him and then who knew what would happen?

"So what are you going to do?" Ali asked.

"I don't know yet," Dev said carefully. "I have to think about it."

Dad nodded slowly. "In the meantime, the reason we are meeting is that Uncle San is getting married." He raised his eyebrows as if to say, *Remember?* "We're going to have the wedding reception in the restaurant, so we need to think about decorations and tablecloths and such."

"There's a wedding store down on Broadway," Dev suggested. "Maybe we could get some ideas there. I could bring Manu. He's awesome at that sort of thing.

He did the decorations for the grade eight dance last spring."

San smiled. "Thank you, Dev. That would be most helpful. I'll ask Parneet which colours she likes best."

"Who's Parneet?" Dev asked. Ali kicked her chair under the table.

"My fiancée," San said.

"Who did you think Parneet was? The new cleaning lady?" Ali giggled.

"Well, how was I supposed to get that?" Dev pretended annoyance. "Gee, information really is on a need-to-know basis around here!"

"Come on," Dad said, "we've got to get moving if we're going to open on time."

Dev wolfed down her neglected *vada,* then rushed to get showered and dressed. By the time she got downstairs, the restaurant kitchen was already steeped in the spicy fragrances of San's cooking.

"Everything smells wonderful," she said, tying on her apron. "San?"

"Yes?" He peeked through the open shelves — full of pepper and cinnamon, cardamom and cayenne — that separated the kitchen from the dishwashing area.

"I'm sorry I made it all about me this morning," Dev said. "I honestly am happy for you."

"No problems." San smiled. "I want you to know that, whatever you decide about the horse, I'm at your back."

"You mean you've *got* my back," Dev corrected gently.

"Yes, and I've got your back, also," San replied gleefully. "But I must warn you: your father will want to talk more about this. The new horse sounds dangerous."

Ali staggered in with a large grey bus pan full of dirty dishes. "All hands on deck," he said and grinned.

"Dishwashing duty calls," Dev agreed.

The job was boring — and she'd done it a million times before — so her mind began to wander. Did she want to learn to cook? Not really. Ali was the one who was always hanging around San asking questions. He was in grade seven, so maybe next year he'd start helping prepare the food.

Did she want this restaurant to be her entire life, like it was her dad's and San's? No. Most definitely, no.

Did she want to take on a horse as frightened as Zim? What would happen to him if she didn't?

What would happen to me?

By the end of the evening, when the last dish was dry and stacked on the stainless-steel counter, Dev had finally found her answer.

5 RUNAWAY!

The next afternoon, Dev arrived at the stables full of purpose, determined to talk to Ms. Caroline first thing, only to find that the stable owner wasn't around. Deflated, Dev went to the tack room to change, then walked the length of the barn to the indoor ring.

The ring was set up for barrel racing. Three oil drums took up the entire ring, one at the north end and two at the south. Elijah, riding Jack, was bolting up the centre toward the north barrel. On Elijah's signal, Jack lowered his head and whipped past it. They flew down the ring to one of the barrels at the south end. Jack danced around it, hind feet digging firmly into the sawdust. Then they raced to the third barrel, hugging it, almost touching it, as they made their final circle. Now they were on the home stretch. Elijah called an encouraging "Ha! Ha!" letting Jack know that all he had to do now was run.

Dev jumped on the fence rail and whooped, "Go Team South Hill!"

Elijah pulled to a stop and his eyes flicked to the clock to check their time. "Atta boy!" he said, leaning down and patting Jack's shoulder. He laid the reins on the side of Jack's neck, and the stocky black horse brought him over to Dev.

"Why, hello, li'l lady," Elijah drawled, tipping an imaginary cowboy hat.

"Hey, how did you do at Burnaby Equestrian's gymkhana? I totally forgot to ask!"

"Third in barrel racing," Elijah said, looking downcast. "That third-place white ribbon is just so, I don't know . . . like something you'd find on a grave."

"Awww," Dev sympathized. "How about the trail class?"

"Only first place," Elijah said, polishing his knuckles on his shirtfront.

"Way to go!"

"You should have been there," Elijah said, barely containing his laughter. "To test obedience, we had to make the horses stand in a row and then eat a piece of carrot cake right in front of their faces."

"That is so mean."

"And the best part was when Quill, that Appaloosa Jeremy Turner rides, just wandered up and stuck his face right in the middle of the cake!"

"Were they disqualified?"

"Outta there!" Elijah reported gleefully. Then he slid down and began leading Jack out of the ring.

Dev opened the gate to let them pass.

"So when will you be able to ride the Glider again?" Elijah asked.

"A few things have happened. I'll fill you in while we clean the stalls."

"Is it your grades?" Elijah undid the cinch on Jack's saddle. "Is your father mad?"

"All will be revealed," she promised.

And as they shovelled, Dev told Elijah everything.

"Wow," he said as they wheeled full barrows out to the manure bin. "So you're really going to try?"

"I've got to." Dev shrugged. "If I want to keep riding, I have no other choice."

"Zim has hardly been out of that stall since he got here, you know. Ms. Caroline's been taking care of him herself. She actually told me not to go in there. It's kind of weird."

"Speaking of Ms. Caroline, do you know where she is?" Dev asked.

"Yeah, she's giving a group lesson in the outdoor ring."

"I wanted to talk to her before I took Zim out, but if she's not around . . ."

"I'd wait if I were you."

"You know what they say: No time like the present. And anyway, he should be used to the place by now." Dev dumped the wheelbarrow forcefully.

They fed all the horses except one. Then Dev

selected an especially tempting chuck of alfalfa, slung a halter over her shoulder, and moved toward Zim's stall.

"Are you sure about this?" Elijah asked.

But Dev, who was already inching open the stall door, didn't answer.

"Okay, then," Elijah said weakly. "I'll be in brushing Jack."

Dev slid into the stall, holding the hay in front of her. "Hey, Big Guy," she crooned, "remember me?"

Zim's head shot up warily.

"Here." Dev moved in one step, then stopped. "Yummy, yummy hay . . ."

Zim moved forward a step, extended his neck, and took a tiny nibble.

"There you go . . ." Dev took a step closer.

Zim's eyes were huge.

Dev held out her arms. "Just a little closer now and I'll —"

Zim snorted, backing away.

"Okay, okay," Dev said soothingly. "Just relax." She dropped the hay and backed up quickly.

The big horse swerved sideways, lightning fast.

Dev jumped for the door but Zim was too fast for her. She'd left it open a crack and one swing of the horse's head flung it wide. He clattered into the hallway and galloped for the main door.

Elijah darted out of Jack's stall with both hands in the air, yelling, "Hyah! Hyah!"

Zim reared, striking the air with his front hooves, then turned and galloped to the indoor ring.

Dev ran after him and grabbed the gate, slamming it just as Zim wheeled toward her. "Gotcha!"

"Good," Elijah said wryly, coming to a stop beside her. "The situation's so totally under control."

They watched Zim bounce around the ring, tail held high, faking and darting away from unseen pursuers. Dev wondered how they were going to catch him.

"We can block off the hallway with . . . I don't know, wheelbarrows," Dev suggested, "and maybe he'll run back into his stall." Zim galloped the length of the ring and jumped clear over an upended oil drum.

"Wheelbarrows, huh?"

"If you've got a better idea, now would be the time to say it."

"I'll saddle up Jack again," Elijah said, "and we'll round him up."

"Round him up?"

"Hey, if *you've* got a better idea . . ."

"Fine." Dev threw up her hands. "We'll round him up."

While she waited for Elijah and Jack, Dev watched Zim in awe. His jumps were powerful, his floating trot breathtaking. Clearly, this magnificent horse loved to move.

Loved being alive.

Elijah led Jack back toward the ring. He had a

length of soft rope coiled over his arm. "When I get this rope around his neck, you're going to have to move fast," Elijah explained. "If Zim won't let me lead him — and I'm guessing he won't — you'll need to jump in and grab him."

"Okay, thanks," Dev said.

"Will you do me a favour?"

"Name it."

"Shut the gate this time?"

Dev nodded sheepishly. "Let me know when you're ready."

Elijah swung into the saddle confidently. "Let's do it."

Dev opened the gate enough to let Elijah and Jack through, then latched it behind them. She clung to the fence, barely daring to breathe.

Jack's ears were forward; he was totally focused. The game was on.

Elijah and Jack chased Zim, horse and rider moving as one, cutting across the ring, zigzagging back and forth like a herd dog. They gave the Arabian less and less space, finally pushing him close to the fence. Then they closed in on him.

Zim was like a car getting cut off in traffic. With the fence on one side and Jack on the other, there was no place to go. He tried stopping and doubling back, but Jack was too fast for him. Wherever he turned, Jack was there.

Zim slowed, then stopped, and Elijah slid the rope around the big horse's neck.

To Dev's amazement, Zim quieted and followed Jack meekly. Dev smiled up at Elijah as she took the rope. "As far as I'm concerned, you guys get the blue ribbon every time."

She led Zim back into his stall, closing the door firmly behind him. She reached up to stroke his sleek neck, glossy red flecked with silver. "You're really something, Zim," she said softly, "but I can't figure out if you're a lion or a lamb." She slipped the rope off his neck and sneaked out the stall door, backing away — straight into Ms. Caroline.

"I can explain," Dev began.

"Don't you have to be somewhere?" Ms. Caroline asked.

It wasn't what Dev was expecting. "I don't . . . what do you . . . ?"

"It's six o'clock? Monday?"

"Omigosh! They're expecting me at the restaurant!"

"You'd better hurry up," Ms. Caroline agreed. "We'll talk later."

"After school tomorrow?"

Ms. Caroline paused. "No, I want you to take a couple of days off. There are some things you need to think about."

Dev's jaw dropped.

"Just think," Ms. Caroline said slowly, "did you learn anything today?" She turned and walked away.

Runaway!

★★★

Dev ran into the tack room, slamming the door behind her. She kicked her rubber boots into the corner and pulled off her coveralls, tossing them carelessly onto a hook. Then she grabbed her bike and, bashing the door open with the wheel, sprinted the length of the hallway. In moments she was through the main gates and gone.

Dev was halfway up Granville Street before she even realized it. Her mind was spinning out of control. Ms. Caroline wanted her to take a couple of days to think about it. What did that even mean? *Am I fired?*

She turned onto 49th Avenue and sped by Ali's school. A shower of blown leaves whirled past, amber and rust red in the deepening darkness. She pulled into the restaurant parking lot and skidded to a stop, then thumped open the storeroom door and let her bike crash to the floor.

"Hurry up!" Ali urged. "Everybody's waiting for you."

"What do you mean, 'everybody'?"

"You know, the party?"

Dev looked at him blankly.

"He means your uncle's engagement party," Dad said, pushing open the door to the dining room. "You'd better get in here."

Dev put her face in her hands. She hoped she didn't reek of manure! She followed her father into the dining room, holding out her hand politely to a woman in a yellow sari. "Hi, I'm Devlin," she said, forcing herself to smile.

San's fiancée stood, beaming, and took Dev's hand. She wasn't as tall as Dev, but she looked strong, fearless. Even though she was wearing traditional clothing — her spangled scarf bounced light everywhere like a glitter ball — she didn't seem very traditional.

"I'm Parneet," the woman said, shaking Dev's hand warmly. "I've been dying to meet you!" She moved closer and whispered, "There are way too many guys in this place. I intend to even things up a bit. You and I? We need to stick together."

"Okay," Dev said uncertainly. Parneet was gorgeous, and definitely confident. Dev could see she was someone who didn't take no for an answer.

"And I understand you're going to help plan the wedding!" Parneet said excitedly. "I can't wait to get started."

6 DREAMS VS. DUTY

Manu was sitting on the school's stair landing, busy wrenching the cover off a plastic bowl. Dev plopped herself beside him. "I missed you this morning." She sighed. "You can't imagine the long, lonely ride of the friendless."

"Sorry," Manu replied. "I had to be in early for a yearbook meeting, Little Miss I-don't-answer-my-messages. What's up with you, anyway?"

"Don't you get mad at me, too," Dev pleaded. "I'm already in trouble with half the known world."

"What's going on?"

"I have to help plan San's stupid wedding and you know I hate that kind of stuff. And I don't know if I'll be able to ride anymore because my science grade is down. And Ms. Caroline's acting like she hates me!"

"Ms. Caroline doesn't hate you, Dev," Manu said. "She made a huge investment in you."

"I don't understand. One minute she's talking about the Canadian Show Jumping Team and the next minute she's telling me to take some time off to think things over. What does she want?"

"The question is, what do *you* want?"

"First, I want to keep riding. That's the main thing. Second, I want to give lessons someday, so I should complete Equine Canada's coaching program. Third, I want to earn a spot on Jump Canada's squad and maybe even get on the Show Jumping Team someday."

"Is that all?" Manu laughed.

"Don't joke. This is important to me."

"Then do whatever it takes to make it happen," Manu said simply.

"Just like that?"

"Just like that," Manu affirmed.

The buzzer went off, signalling the end of lunch, so Dev and Manu both had to cram down the rest of their food.

"Listen, I need a huge favour," Dev said, chewing. "San's fiancée wants me to go with her to Bells on Broadway after school today."

"Are they going to do the full-out Indian thing? Is San going to ride in on an elephant?"

"We're Catholic, so no," Dev said, getting up and slinging on her backpack. "But what I wanted to ask you was, will you come with me today? You'd better say yes, because I already volunteered you."

"Wouldn't miss it," Manu called as Dev started downstairs. "Meet me at my locker!"

Her next class was science. More physics, which just seemed to Dev a sneaky way to get them to do extra math. The blackboard was covered with lines and arrows meant to represent energy and forces: combining forces, balanced forces, acceleration, friction . . .

Who cares? Dev thought.

Mr. Davies talked about how physics related to engineering, and how everything around them, including the building they were sitting in, had been engineered. He told them that Canadian engineers wore iron rings, originally made from a bridge that had fallen down. The rings reminded them what would happen if they didn't do a good job. That the people a roof caved in on could die. That the workers building a bridge could die.

"Engineers = rings = responsibility," Dev wrote in her notes.

Responsibility, she mused. *I guess if I take over Zim's training, he'll be my responsibility. I wonder what my ring should be made of?*

Dev had to pay attention again.

"I want you to look up the Ironworkers Memorial Bridge," Mr. Davies said, "and write a paragraph on the origin of its name."

"It used to be called the Second Narrows Bridge," Jason Freeman volunteered.

"Thank you," Mr. Davies said, nodding. "So when was it renamed and why?"

Dev wrote that down as the buzzer sounded. Then

she clapped her book shut and headed to social studies.

Mr. Altan reminded them of their local history project, which was due in a month. Dev still hadn't picked a topic. *Maybe I should write about the Ironworkers Memorial Bridge,* she thought. *Reduce, reuse, recycle!*

She was relieved when the final bell rang and it was time to meet Manu.

"Thank you for doing this," Dev said. "I really owe you one."

"Why? Is San marrying the Wicked Witch of the West or something?"

"No, she's fine, I guess," Dev said. "I don't know."

"Your enthusiasm is underwhelming. C'mon, we can take the bike route the whole way there."

They arrived at the store and locked their bikes outside. Parneet came to meet them before they even had their helmets off.

"Uh, Parneet, I'd like you to meet my friend Manu," Dev said.

"Great!" Parneet smiled. "Any friend of Devlin's is a friend of mine."

Manu clapped his hands together eagerly. "Parneet, have you decided on colours?"

"I was thinking of a fall theme, you know, since it is autumn," Parneet said.

"Good idea." Manu nodded. "Reds and yellows. Nice."

Dev thought she might pass out from boredom.

"So are you big on the streamers-and-bells thing?" Manu asked. "Because if not, I know a place to get stuff that might be a bit more fun."

"Let's go!" Parneet said.

Dev felt like her eyes were stuffed full the second she stepped into the store. Parneet and Manu started rushing around grabbing silk flowers and tablecloths. Dev was wandering up an aisle, looking at an amazing variety of gift bags, when she crashed into someone.

"Sorry about that," Dev said, then, "Oh, hi!" It was Jenn.

"Dev! Hi! What are you doing here?"

"Getting decorations for my uncle's wedding. How about you?"

"My sister's birthday is next week. Hey, I want you to meet my mom." Before Dev could say anything, Jenn grabbed her mother's arm and dragged her over. "This is Dev from South Hill. She rides Mirror Glider."

"I've seen you jump and it's pretty thrilling," Jenn's mom said. "You have to be fearless to excel at that sport."

Dev smiled. "If you trust your horse, there's nothing to worry about."

"Well, it's lovely to meet you! Jenn talks about you all the time."

"Nice to meet you, too."

With a tiny wave, Jenn's mother moved up the aisle. Jenn hung back. "Listen," she began, "I've been meaning to talk to you. I'm sorry I didn't say anything when Anna was ordering you guys around. You know, after the show?"

Like I need reminding. "Doesn't matter. Elijah and I are the stablehands, after all."

"No." Jenn shook her head, smiling. "You're more than that. You both are. The way you are with the horses . . ." She looked over her shoulder and winced. "I'd better go. My mom probably needs me to carry a ton of helium balloons or something."

"Okay, bye." Dev walked slowly to the end of the row, batting Jenn's words around her mind. *You're more than that.* She tried to see where Jenn was making fun of her, or putting her down. But she couldn't.

Manu ran around the corner and grabbed her arm. "You have to see this!" he said breathlessly.

They caught up with Parneet, whose arms were full of long-stemmed flowers.

With a *ta-da* flourish, Manu gestured toward an arch woven of burgundy twigs. "This would be so fun," he said. "We could put it behind the head table to sort of define the space."

"How do you know all this stuff?" Dev marvelled.

"I just go with my gut," Manu said. "It's not rocket science."

"Or engineering," Dev joked, and at that exact second, she noticed an iron ring on Parneet's finger. "Parneet! Are you an engineer?"

"Yes, a mechanical engineer —" Parneet smiled "— although at present, I'm teaching physics at Langara College."

"Physics, eh? Have I got a job for you." Manu grinned, draping his arm around Dev's shoulders.

"Let's talk over coffee," Parneet said. "I am exhausted now."

"Should we get the arch?" Manu asked hopefully.

"Yes, bring it," Parneet said, laughing.

They piled the counter high.

After manhandling the arch into the back of Parneet's car, Dev and Manu collapsed in a corner booth at the Second Cup. Parneet got hot drinks and brought them over. "So what's this about a job for me?" she asked as she sat down.

"Someone who shall not be named could use a little help with science," Manu said.

Dev elbowed him playfully. "It's true," she admitted. "I'm a big failure."

"You're not a failure," Parneet said. "You just need more support. I have noticed . . . oh, I shouldn't say."

Dev sat forward. "I want to hear."

"It's just that your father's plans for you don't line up with *your* plans. You need to focus on your own dreams."

Dev felt mystified. "Isn't that disloyal?"

"When I decided to be an engineer, my parents freaked out and started yelling, 'What kind of woman does that? It's not feminine!' But I did it anyway and now they brag to everyone. I think they actually believe it was their idea!"

"I do have dreams," Dev said softly, "but I don't know what to do about them."

"I'll help you, if you want," Parneet said. "I have some ideas."

Dev grinned. "I need all the help I can get!"

"Well, hiring more staff for the kitchen is one of my ideas. I'm buying a part ownership of the restaurant, so I'll have a say in hiring decisions. Besides, we're all going to be family very soon."

"Yeah, about that . . . how did you meet Uncle Santhosh?" Dev loved her uncle, but San marrying a mechanical-engineer-college-instructor seemed weird.

"We met through a marriage registry," Parneet explained. "They didn't want to match us at first because our education levels are so different, but I insisted on meeting him."

"Really? Why?"

"What do you mean, why?" Parneet exclaimed.

"Well, it's just that," Dev stammered, "he's only a cook."

Manu gave her a look.

"Only a cook!" Parneet shook her head. "A man who can cook is at the top of my list. Plus —" she ticked off the points on her fingers "— he's tall, handsome, intelligent, sweet . . ."

"Okay, okay, I get it!" Dev laughed and threw up her hands.

"Finally," Parneet continued slowly, "a man who leaves his home and comes to a foreign place to help his brother raise two children is someone I'll always be able to count on."

7 STEPPING UP

I slide open a stall door at South Hill. It's dark and cold, the air misty. The floor is covered with dirty straw and manure. I step in, instantly knee-deep in filth. It's like wading through mud. It's quicksand, pulling me down.

In the corner, in the shadows, I see movement. Zim, wearing a bridle of reddish leather and a gleaming English saddle, steps out of the darkness. He stares at me.

He's so sad it makes me want to cry. The way he looks. Full of longing. He needs something. What?

I'm almost under. The choking straw fills my mouth. I can't see. Can't breathe. I reach up blindly. The reins fall into my hand. I hold on.

Zim is backing up, pulling steadily, the whites of his eyes showing. Fierce and terrible.

I'm still holding on when I hear Ms. Caroline's voice. "Did you learn anything today?"

Dev shuddered and woke up, rocking back on the desk chair in her room. She tried to force herself to focus on the math worksheet that was due that day. She checked her alarm clock for what seemed like the millionth time. It was seven a.m. She dialed a number on her cell phone.

"South Hill Stables," Ms. Caroline answered sleepily.

"Hi, Ms. Caroline, it's me," Dev said in a rush. "I'm sorry to call so early but I figured it out!"

"Figured what out?"

"What you wanted me to learn! Zim's not wild! He's been trained!"

"I also would have accepted 'Don't sneak up on a horse and scare the living daylights out of him,'" Ms. Caroline said. "But your answer is good, too. Why do you think that?"

"As soon as Elijah got the lead rope around his neck, Zim was fine. He walked right beside me and went straight into his stall. He knows how to jump, too! You should have seen him."

"Does that mean you're going to take him on?"

"Yes," Dev said. "Ms. Caroline, I want to be someone you can count on."

"You *are* someone I count on. I wouldn't have asked you to do this unless I thought you could."

"He has a lot of potential, doesn't he?

"So do you."

Dev floated through the schoolday, waiting for the three-fifteen buzzer. Then she whipped over to her locker and dumped her textbooks inside.

"Oh my," Manu said, frowning, "and where might we be going in such a hurry?"

"South Hill," Dev said.

"I thought you were taking some time off to think."

"I did. I thought," Dev said. "I decided I want to train Zim."

"Shouldn't you talk to your dad about this?"

"Nope." Dev motioned Manu away impatiently. "Move."

"But the wedding thingies," Manu said, flapping his hands in the shape of a table arrangement. "We're supposed to be getting everything ready."

Dev looked at her watch. "Okay, let's meet at my place at five-thirty and we'll organize like there's no tomorrow."

"Ahem." Manu raised his eyebrows, opened Dev's locker, and pulled out her science textbook. "You might want to bring this, too." He handed the book over.

Pedalling fast, Dev flew along 41st Avenue, down Granville, then beside the mighty Fraser. The river glimmered jade in the cold light. Dev shivered as a chill wind blew past her, followed by a shower of rain. She arrived at the stable and wheeled her bike inside, grateful for the warmth of the barn and its familiar scents of leather and hay.

She poked her head into Ms. Caroline's office. "Hey!"

"Dev!" Ms. Caroline greeted her. "I didn't expect to see you today."

"I just wanted to talk to you and maybe spend some time with our little jailbreaker."

Ms. Caroline laughed. "Great. Come on."

"I'd like to move Mirror Glider into the stall beside Zim," Dev explained as they walked through the stable. "I think she'd be a good influence on him."

"Okay," Ms. Caroline agreed, "but the space on the other side of him should stay empty. He's still a nervous young horse."

They looked into Zim's stall. He was standing in the dark, in the farthest possible corner.

"For now, I want to keep a halter on him all the time," Dev said. "A soft one, with sheepskin over the nose strap so he won't be uncomfortable."

"Are you sure that's a good idea?"

"Call it an experiment. I think it will make him feel more secure, like he belongs to someone." Dev remembered her dream and the terrible loneliness she'd sensed in Zim. "I think he needs a new herd."

Dev went into the tack room and looped a blue halter over her right arm. Ms. Caroline opened Zim's stall door a crack and slid inside. Dev followed, latching the door firmly behind her.

"C'mon, Zim," Ms. Caroline called soothingly. "Everything's going to be all right."

Dev walked slowly to Zim's left shoulder, then inched her hand toward him. "Good boy," she crooned. "Stand still for me, Big Guy."

She let the halter slide down her arm until it made contact with Zim's neck. Then she moved closer, slipping the strap under his chin with her other hand. Finally, she skimmed the nose strap forward, nervous he'd pull away, and inched it up past his muzzle.

To her relief, Zim lowered his nose obediently and let Dev buckle the halter. "That's right," she said, stroking her hand along his neck. "Looks like you need a little grooming, yes you do. Next time, I'll bring some brushes and . . ."

Zim dipped his head and nuzzled Dev's hand.

"He likes you," Ms. Caroline whispered.

"I like him, too." Dev moved her fingers up Zim's cheek affectionately, then clipped a lead rope to the ring of his halter. "Can I take him out?"

"Sure. Just remember to take things slowly."

Dev positioned herself beside Zim's head and clicked her tongue, telling him to walk. Zim moved forward two steps and stopped, right at the door of his stall.

Dev realized he was shaking. "You can do this," she encouraged him. "You don't have to be scared."

Very slowly, Zim put one foot forward.

"Walk," Dev said firmly.

Zim inched into the hallway.

"Good boy," Dev said as Zim fell into step beside her. She led him out the front door into a curtain of drizzle.

Zim twitched, crowding her.

"Hey," Dev gently pushed his head away. "Walk!"

Zim shimmied backward.

"Stop," Dev warned.

Zim wheeled away.

"No! Quit it!" Dev shouted. She kept a tight grip on the rope and firmly pulled his head toward her. "We go back when I say."

Zim stopped.

Dev took a deep breath, signalled Zim to walk, and turned him back to the stable. *I'm not sure this counts as a victory,* she mused as she let him back into his stall, *but it's a start.*

★★★

Dev had to motor to get home on time. She dumped her bike in the storeroom and flew up the stairs.

Manu was already in the kitchen, admiring a huge stack of silk leaves, a riot of scarlet and gold. Bottle-green vases gleamed along the counter.

"Wow, I didn't realize we bought so much stuff!" Dev called, heaving her backpack to the floor. She went into the bathroom to wash her hands, then hurried back to the kitchen.

Manu was quickly picking stalks from the stack and organizing them by size and colour.

"You don't actually need me, do you?" Dev said, feeling deflated.

"Not yet."

Dev sat down with a sigh.

"Isn't there something you should be doing, home-work-wise?" asked Manu.

Dev stuck out her tongue, then retrieved her back-pack and dragged it to the table. She pulled out her science book, opened it, and began to read.

On the second page of the physics chapter, there was a large shaded box about the Ironworkers Memorial Bridge. "Check this out," she told Manu. "We're supposed to research this bridge and the information's right here in the textbook. What do you bet half the class will whine that they couldn't find anything?"

"Ha," Manu snorted, "except for Jason Freeman. He'll show up with a working model and a ten-page report!"

"You know, that tragedy was caused by a failure in communication," Parneet said. Dev hadn't even heard her come in.

"You mean, like, the carrier pigeons went off course?" Dev said.

"Very funny." Parneet shook her head, smiling. "It wasn't that long ago. It was 1958. Two different engin-eering firms worked on the project, one starting from each side of the Narrows." Parneet tented her hands, fingertips almost touching. "But they didn't talk to each other enough. The crane they used to support the centre wasn't able to bear the weight." Parneet let her hands fall. "And so, collapse."

Dev could imagine it clearly. Men falling, scream-ing. Trying to grab hold of something, anything. Then hitting the water. Going so deep there was only dark-ness. No way to get to the surface.

Why did the ironworkers have to pay for somebody else's mistake? she wondered. Why did some people have to work in the dirt while others stayed inside, all warm and comfortable?

"Dev?" Parneet asked. "Did I lose you?"

"There are a lot of things I don't understand." Dev sighed.

Parneet pulled out a chair and sat down. "About physics?"

Dev shrugged.

"Think of it this way," Parneet said. "When you're rid-ing a horse, what do you do when you go over a jump?"

"I lean forward."

"What would happen if you didn't?"

Dev laughed. "I'd flip right off the horse's rear end!"

"Why?"

"Because . . . I don't know." Dev shrugged again.

"When the horse begins to jump, he exerts an ac-celeration force, forward and up," Parneet explained.

"So I move forward . . ."

". . . to create a combined force instead of an op-posing one."

Dev pictured a group of lines and arrows repre-senting a horse and rider going over a jump, and it all didn't seem so useless anymore. "When you think of it that way, it's pretty amazing," Dev marvelled. "I mean, how does the horse know how hard to jump?"

"You mean how much force to apply? Experience," Parneet said, "and lots of practice. Oh, that reminds me — I talked to your father about you."

"What do you mean?"

"Would you like to take a break from dishwashing? I think you need time to focus on this new horse —" Parneet raised one eyebrow "— and perhaps also your studies."

"Can I do that?"

"Easily! Do you mind if we hire a new dishwasher?"

Dev sat back in her chair, flooded with relief. "I don't mind at all," she said. "Thank you!"

"You can thank her by tying ribbons around these," Manu said, pointing to a row of glass vases.

With each swatch of cloth she tied, Dev felt happier. No more cleaning up people's half-eaten food! No more sweating over an old dishwasher that belonged in a museum! She'd finally have some time to herself!

Time to do what she wanted to do.

All of the centrepieces were finished. "This is really great, Manu!" Parneet said. "San and I were wondering, also, if you would be our wedding photographer."

"Me?" Manu gulped.

"We'd pay you, of course. Your first official photography job."

"He's an awesome photographer," Dev said, delighted. "He even manages to make *me* look good."

"Oh, please." Parneet rolled her eyes. "Like that's hard, with that complexion and those green eyes."

"You're not so bad yourself," Dev said.

And she meant it.

8 OUT OF THE SHADOWS

Dev slipped into Zim's stall, latching the door behind her. "Hi, Zim," she whispered. "Hey, Big Guy, it's me."

Zim stood in the corner with his hindquarters to her, swishing his tail.

"You don't want to come see me? Don't want to see what I have?"

Zim tossed his head and snorted.

"Okay, maybe our friend Mirror Glider wants what I have." Dev slipped out of Zim's stall and into Mirror Glider's.

The big grey came right up, swishing her soft lips across Dev's hand and taking the treat. "Yeah, that's right," Dev said, patting the Glider's neck. "A crunchy carrot."

Zim came closer, eyeing them through the planks that separated the stalls.

Dev made a big fuss over Mirror Glider, stroking her mane. "I'll have to get the brushes and Tail Shine and give you a little attention, won't I?" She heard Zim come a step closer and glanced over her shoulder.

Zim was resting his muzzle awkwardly on the top rail.

Dev pulled another carrot from her back pocket and poked it into Zim's mouth. He took it in one bite and skipped back to the other side of the stall, crunching contentedly.

"Let's look at that hoof." Crouching at the Glider's shoulder, Dev touched the inside of the mare's knee. Mirror Glider lifted her foot obediently, revealing a shiny new shoe.

"Looks like Ms. Caroline had you shod again," Dev rattled on. "What do you say we take these babies for a test drive?"

The Glider rubbed her head against Dev almost like she was nodding.

Dev went to the tack room and got a pail of brushes, hanging it from the crook of her arm. Then she draped the Glider's bridle over her shoulder and balanced her English saddle, complete with its cushy saddle pad, on her forearm.

She pulled the Glider's stall door open with her free hand and set down the pail and saddle in one corner. She didn't bother closing the stall door. *Never in a million years would this horse run away from me,* she thought, shaking her head. *I'm really going to miss the old girl.*

Standing on the Glider's left, Dev held up the bridle with one hand, supporting the snaffle bit with the other. A soon as Dev touched the bit to the Glider's lips, the horse accepted it and let Dev slide the bridle over her ears and buckle it under her chin.

Dev pulled the Glider's forelock over the top strap and tugged on it affectionately. She sprayed Tail Shine on the Glider's silver mane, sliding the stiff brush through it. Then Dev took the currycomb and combed the big mare from the crest of her neck to her hocks. Finally, she did it all again with the soft brush, working down Mirror Glider's legs to her dark hooves.

Taking the saddle with both hands, Dev heaved it onto the mare's back, making sure it was well up on her withers. She swung the stirrup out of the way and did up the girth, sliding her hand underneath the strap to make sure it didn't pinch.

Dev knew that Zim had been watching them the whole time, peeking through the rails, never taking his eyes off her. *What a strange animal,* she mused, *so unfriendly, yet so lonely.*

"Let's go." She began to lead Mirror Glider out of the stall.

Zim nickered softly.

"Oh, did you want to come, too?" Dev asked, feigning surprise.

Dev let the Glider's reins drop. The grey stood obediently in front of Zim's stall as Dev got a coiled rope from the tack room.

"Want to go for a jog, Big Guy?" Dev opened Zim's door cautiously. To her relief, Zim stood still as she clipped the rope to his halter.

Dev took a deep breath as she walked Zim into the hallway. *You have to be ready for anything with this one.* She picked up the Glider's reins and led both horses to the end of the hall.

She let the Glider's reins drop again as she opened the gate. Keeping a firm grip on Zim, Dev brought him into the indoor ring and tied him to the middle fence rail. Then she led in Mirror Glider and shut the gate firmly. She pulled down the stirrup, put her boot in it, and swung on.

By the time she and the Glider turned back to Zim, he was free. He had undone the knot with his lips! Dev could have sworn he was grinning as he ran off with his tail in the air.

"You got us again!" Dev called to him. "Whatever shall we do? Oh, yeah. Catch you."

She and the Glider caught up with Zim easily, cantering by his side. Then Dev leaned over and seized the trailing rope with one swift movement.

Zim instantly fell into step behind them, echoing the Glider exactly, cantering, trotting, then walking.

"You're such a good boy," Dev crooned. "A little nuts maybe, but still a good boy."

"I see you've tamed the wild beast!" Elijah shouted from the hallway. "Way to go!"

"Not quite," Dev replied with a grin. "He's still difficult one minute, then willing the next."

"At least he's not boring!"

"Definitely not," Dev agreed. "Hey, will you do me a favour?"

"Sure." Elijah climbed between the fence rails and into the ring.

"Will you take the Glider in for me? I want to spend a bit more time with this one while he's in a good mood."

Still hanging on to Zim's rope, Dev jumped off Mirror Glider and handed the reins over.

"Are you going to put him on a lunge line?" Elijah asked as he brought Mirror Glider out of the ring.

"No, I think going around in circles will get old pretty fast," Dev said. "I'd rather run with him."

"I'll stand by with the first-aid kit."

Dev watched Elijah lead Mirror Glider back to her stall. *Good old Elijah,* she thought. *I owe him one. Maybe a thousand and one.* She turned her attention to Zim, who was standing quietly with his head down.

"Okay, Mystery Man, let's see what you can do." She shortened her hold on the lead rope and bunched the rest in her other hand, being careful not to loop it around her fingers.

She pulled gently on the lead, clicking twice with her tongue. Zim started walking beside her, turning his head toward her happily.

Dev broke into a slow run, signalling to him again. Zim eased into a trot. Then Dev started running faster and Zim's trot extended into the spectacular float that only Arabian horses can do. They ran around the ring six times until Dev had to slow down, finally coming to a gentle stop.

Zim snorted at her.

"Easy for you to say," Dev panted. "You're a horse and I'm just a feeble human. Come on. It's time for a change of scenery."

Dev walked Zim to the outside gate. It had been raining hard all day, but now a red-orange blaze was streaming from the sky's edge. Dev swung the gate wide and brought Zim through it.

Zim paused where the roof ended and suddenly shied.

"Hey, hey," Dev said soothingly. "What are you afraid of?" She settled him down, then signalled him to start walking again.

Zim backed up, pulling away.

"Don't do that," Dev warned.

The whites of Zim's eyes were showing.

"Stop!" Dev yelled firmly. "Quit it!"

But Zim reared and struck out with both front feet.

Dev twisted away, still holding the rope, and fell face down in a huge puddle.

If Ms. Caroline could see me now, Dev thought. She pushed herself into a sitting position, then got up wearily, completely soaked.

Zim was staring at her with huge eyes. He looked

completely amazed, like he couldn't believe she was there.

"Yup, I'm waterproof," Dev said.

Zim took a step forward and butted Dev with his head. It seemed like he was saying: *Are you real?*

"Yeah, I'm real," she sighed. "Real muddy, thanks to you."

Zim moved his head down to Dev's feet, then up to her face.

"Are you happy now?"

Very slowly, very gently, Zim rubbed his lips across Dev's cheek.

She pressed her face against his neck, laughing, "Okay, okay. I'm glad to see you, too. But for now, we have to go inside. I'm freezing."

As they made their way back to his stall, Zim kept turning his head toward Dev. Over and over, he stopped and stared at her, then continued walking, bobbing his head happily.

They passed Elijah in the hallway. He opened his mouth and shut it again.

"Don't ask," Dev said.

"Do you want me to . . ."

"Don't worry about it. I'll look after him." Dev brought Zim into his stall, brushed him down, and fed him.

Elijah was oiling his saddle when Dev slumped into the tack room. She sat on the floor to pull off her muddy boots.

"Heck of a day, eh?" Elijah gave her a sympathetic look.

"I think we made progress, though, in our own way."

Elijah heaved his saddle onto the storage rack. "Too bad about the water thing."

"What do you mean?"

"I saw what happened out there, Dev. He was scared of a puddle!"

"Is that what it was? Do you think it's a deal breaker?"

"He can't be a show jumper if he shies every time he sees water." Elijah shrugged.

"Yeah," Dev said sadly. "You know, we need to find out what happened to him."

"Well, Jerry said he came from the SPCA. Want me to try calling them?"

Dev nodded. She crept to the office and opened the door a crack. "Nobody here," she whispered, waving Elijah over. She turned on the tiny desk lamp as Elijah flipped through the business cards on Ms. Caroline's desk.

"Success!" Elijah squinted at a card and dialed. "Uh, yes," he said after a moment. "This is Jerry Frederick from South Hill Stables. We adopted a horse from you about six weeks ago ..."

Dev could hear a voice squeaking on the other end of the line.

"That's right, Zim," Elijah continued, motioning for

a pen. "We've run into some odd behaviour, and we were wondering if you could tell us any more about him."

Dev tucked a pen into Elijah's hand.

"Dr. Christiansen, a veterinarian. Thank you very much." Elijah wrote down a phone number, then looked up at Dev. "Zim was brought in by a vet!"

"Weird."

Elijah dialed again. "Yes, hello," he said. "Is Dr. Christiansen available?"

Dev could hardly stand the suspense.

"Sure. This is Jerry Frederick from South Hill. We adopted the horse Dr. Christiansen donated to the SPCA, and we have a few questions."

Elijah listened. Then he slowly placed the phone in its cradle.

"What?" Dev demanded.

"Dr. Christiansen wasn't there, only his office assistant. She said Zim should have been put down."

"Put down?" Dev gasped. "Killed?"

"She said Dr. Christiansen wanted to give Zim a chance because he's only four years old. Then she told me not to call again and hung up on me!"

"You're kidding."

"She acted like they did something wrong, keeping Zim alive."

Dev shook her head in disbelief.

"Something's not right here," Elijah said. "Dev, she sounded scared."

9 TRAGEDY ON BURNABY MOUNTAIN

Dev's dad pounded on her door. "Family meeting!"

"Okay! Almost finished!" Dev called. She checked her science assignment to make sure she hadn't missed anything. She hadn't. She slipped it into her backpack.

She stopped by the fridge on the way to the table to grab a jug of milk. Ali carried over a wobbly stack of buttered toast as San dropped scrambled eggs onto everyone's plates.

After saying the speediest grace known to man, Dad launched the meeting. "Okay, we all know the wedding's coming up soon. Even though you're not working these days, Dev, I'll need you to —"

"Not working at the restaurant," Dev corrected him. "I still work at South Hill." She didn't know why she needed to make that point but it seemed important somehow.

"Not working at the restaurant," Dad repeated, "but I'll need you to serve at the reception and clear dishes. I also want to talk to you before you leave for school."

"No problem," she said, but her eggs stuck a little on the way down.

"Ali, you'll show everyone to their seats and help your sister with the serving."

Ali flashed a peace sign, munching his toast.

"And San is not allowed to do anything! It's his party and he needs to relax. Is that understood?" Without waiting for an answer, Dad stood up and walked into the living room. Dev followed meekly.

"So," he began, "I understand you want to work in a barn instead of with your family."

"Dad, that's not fair."

"I thought you were giving it up. And then I find out you're working with this bad animal."

Who blabbed? It took Dev about a nanosecond to realize it must have been Manu.

"Do you know why I let you stop your job here?" Dad continued. "So you could put time into your studies!"

"And work at South Hill!" Dev protested. "That's what Parneet said."

"You misunderstood."

"You're the one who doesn't understand, Dad! Ms. Caroline thinks I could be in the Olympics someday. She believes in me. Why don't you?"

Dev ran, stopping only to grab her stuff. She shrugged on her backpack as she pushed her bike out the door.

"Hi." Manu waved.

But Dev was already pedalling up 49th Avenue.

"What?" Manu sputtered, speeding after her. "What did I do?"

"Did you tell my dad about Zim?" Dev glared at her friend. "That I'm training him?"

"He'd have to be brain-dead not to know! You're never home anymore!" Manu scowled. "Why didn't you talk to him about it?"

"Because he wouldn't have let me, okay? Because he thinks everything I do is a waste of time."

"He does not think that." Manu rolled his eyes.

They rode onto the school grounds through the corner gate and cut across the field. Dev jumped off her bike and shoved it into the rack.

"Don't be mad, please?" Manu begged. "He asked me. What was I supposed to do? Lie? You know it's impossible to lie to your dad."

"I guess."

"It was like being questioned by the cops! I'm lucky to still have my —"

"Too much information!"

"I was going to say 'pride,' you sicko."

"Sorry," Dev said. "I shouldn't have been so mean. Especially today, when I need your help."

"When *don't* you need my help, old buddy old pal?" Manu backed away, bowing.

"Meet me in the library at noon," Dev called after

him. "We need to do some research!" She walked to science class, slid into her seat, and opened her binder to her completed bridge assignment.

Mr. Davies was fiddling with the projector. "Are we all here?" he asked. "Good. Now, the Ironworkers Memorial Bridge. Let's hear from somebody different today. How about you, Devlin?"

Dev sat up straight. "It's . . . um . . . actually the second bridge to be built on that spot. The first one fell in 1958."

"Right. Why?"

"It was a failure of communication —" Dev cleared her throat "— between the engineers. A couple of different firms worked on it, starting from each side of the Narrows. But the middle crane that one company ordered wasn't strong enough to support the whole weight. The bridge was almost finished when it just crumpled and fell. Eighteen ironworkers died in the accident."

"Outstanding!" Mr. Davies said. "How about you, Jennifer? When was the current one built?"

Jenn beamed at Dev. "Well, as Dev said, the first bridge fell in 1958, and then . . ."

Dev returned Jenn's smile before slumping back in relief. *Thank you, Parneet!* She was happy to hear Jenn taking up where she had left off, building on her answer. *And thank you, Jenn. The next time there's a group project, count me in.* When she handed in her assignment at the end of class, Mr. Davies actually smiled.

In social studies, Mr. Altan reminded them of their history project due date. "Oh, and I won't accept anything on a certain bridge collapse," he said breezily. "Just FYI."

Rats. Disappointment fluttered through the class.

"Now, where were we? Ah, yes, British Columbia, the early years . . ."

When the buzzer went, Dev slipped her binder into her backpack and took off. If she and Manu didn't get to the library first, they wouldn't snag a computer.

Manu was already there, logged in and ready to go. "It pays to have friends in high places," he said.

Dev pulled her chair closer so they could see the same screen. "Where do we start?"

"It depends," Manu said slowly, "on what you're looking for."

"I need to find out what happened with Zim. Elijah made some calls. He found out Zim was supposed to be put down, but the vet couldn't do it."

Manu thought a moment. "Let's start with the newspaper archive. We can access it through the library databases."

"The what?"

Manu gave her a pitying look and began to type. "Do you know how long he was at the SPCA before coming to South Hill?"

"Two months, give or take. And he's been at South Hill about seven weeks."

"Right. So if something happened, it was probably around four months ago." Manu typed in the date range and the word "horse."

"That's it?"

"Watch and learn."

Results tumbled down the page. "Horse show . . . jumping . . . Dev Rani the big winner . . ." Manu mumbled. "Look! Here." He clicked on a link.

A news story filled the screen. The headline was "Tragedy on Burnaby Mountain." Dev leaned over and scrolled down, reading:

Tragedy struck yesterday when a horse slid off a popular Burnaby Mountain riding trail into a flooded bog. The rider, 14-year-old Janine Miller, became trapped under the horse and died at the scene. Record rainfall has made marshes at the foot of the mountain hazardous, and the trail is now closed. A spokesperson for the Burnaby Equestrian Association blamed the Parks Board's poor maintenance of the . . .

Then Dev scrolled to a photograph of a blond girl in English riding gear posing with her stunning Arabian: *Zim*.

She felt like crying. She could picture the whole thing. Zim's hind foot sliding into the mud. Falling.

Thrashing. Trying to get up. And the whole time, the girl was stuck under him, stuck in the water. "Poor Janine," Dev said. "She drowned. She *died,* Manu."

So that's why Zim was shocked when I climbed out of that puddle! He was relieved I was still alive!

"Manu! Zim thinks it's his fault."

"He's not the only one," Manu announced grimly. He flipped back to the search results and clicked on the headline: "Equestrian Association protests killing." The article began:

The Burnaby Equestrian Association is protesting Ron and Paula Miller's decision to destroy the horse they say caused their daughter's death . . .

"That's enough," Dev said, turning away. "I can't take this all in right now."

Manu printed out the articles and handed them over. "For your socials project," he said. "Hey, it's local history."

"Thanks. Thank you." Dev put the printouts in her backpack. "Listen, I'm going to take off. I want to go to the barn."

"Not advisable."

"And if Dad finds out, someone might lose more than his pride. Just FYI."

"I know nothing."

"Later," Dev said, then stepped into the crowded hallway and was gone.

★★★

The familiar route blurred past. She rode her bike to the back of the stable and leaned it against an old wagon wheel. Then she slid the barn door open a crack and snuck inside.

Ms. Caroline was in her office, yelling at Jerry. Dev flipped open the door to Zim's stall and hid inside.

"How could you tip off that sneak at the vet's office? You know Christiansen and I had a deal!"

"I don't know what you're talking about," Jerry answered. "I would never . . ."

"Whatever," Ms. Caroline said. "Don't bother. It's too late now, anyway."

"I'd love to know what you think I did."

"Someone named Jerry Frederick called the vet's office last week looking for information about Zim."

"No."

"Yes. And that partner of his, Evelyn Dickson, heard the whole thing. She called the Millers and now they're threatening to sue Christiansen and South Hill."

"I swear, Caroline! I swear I didn't make that call."

"Well, somebody did, and now we're in a world of hurt."

Zim snuffled the top of Dev's head, then rested his

chin on her shoulder. Dev reached up to stroke his nose.

"What are you going to do?" Jerry asked.

"Try to talk them out of it. I left a message for Ron Miller and he's supposed to —"

The phone shrilled, as if on cue.

"South Hill Stables," Ms. Caroline said in her nicest voice. "Oh, yes. Thank you for calling back, Mr. Miller. I wanted to talk about . . . I know, and I'm so sorry, but please understand there's another girl here who's been working very hard . . . She's doing so well . . . Mr. Miller?"

Dev heard Ms. Caroline put down the phone.

"He won't listen, Jerry. He says we have to give Zim back."

Dev pressed her face to Zim's and cried.

10 FIGHTING FOR ZIM'S LIFE

Dev flipped through the pages of her science book, trying to study. She hadn't been able to focus on anything since she'd overheard the argument at the barn. She couldn't bring herself to ask Ms. Caroline about it. Couldn't even talk to Elijah about it.

"What's going on?" Parneet laid her hand on Dev's shoulder. "I thought we were working on chemistry problems today."

Dev looked down, afraid she might start crying again. "Sorry, I'll try to pull it together."

"No. Tell me."

"Elijah and I did something wrong," Dev said falteringly, "well, kind of wrong. But only because we wanted to help Zim!"

"What did you do?"

"We wanted to find out where Zim came from, and what happened to make him so scared of everything. We made some phone calls and Elijah sort of pretended to be somebody else."

"Sort of pretended?"

"He said he was Jerry, Ms. Caroline's partner at South Hill."

"That was probably a bad idea, but it doesn't seem like a huge crime to me."

"The problem is, we called the vet who donated Zim to the SPCA and somebody heard."

"You lost me," Parneet said.

"The vet was supposed to put Zim down but he didn't. He couldn't. He gave Zim to the SPCA so Ms. Caroline could adopt him."

"Why was the horse supposed to be euthanized? Is he sick?"

"No, there was an accident. A bad one. A girl died."

"And people believe it was Zim's fault."

Dev nodded, unable to speak.

"Was it his fault?" Parneet looked at her searchingly.

"No, it wasn't. But now they know Zim's still alive and they're threatening to sue Ms. Caroline. They say we have to give Zim back so they can put him down!"

"You've been spending a lot of time with him, haven't you?"

"I'm the only one who feeds him now. I exercise him and take care of him every day. He likes me, Parneet. I'm finally starting to get through to him."

Parneet looked thoughtful. "The problem is, if the owners paid to have the horse euthanized and then he wasn't, it's basically fraud."

"I don't care about that," Dev wailed. "He's only four years old. None of this is fair!"

"You're right. It's not fair," Parneet agreed. "Wait — what did you mean you're 'starting to get through to him'?"

"He's afraid of water," Dev admitted, "but I'm working on it. I'm making progress."

"Is that what caused the accident? His fear of water?"

"I'm pretty sure his fear is *because* of the accident."

"I see. Listen, my brother is a lawyer. I'm going to call him. Maybe he can help."

Dev wiped her face on her sleeve. "Thank you so much, Parneet."

"In the meantime, you need to work on this fear problem. You have to show that Zim is not a danger to anyone. It's his only chance."

Dev nodded.

"Be firm with him. Show him he has to do it your way."

"You mean like tough love?"

"Yes. To save his life."

Dev sneaked a glance at the kitchen clock. "Do you mind if we quit for tonight, Parneet? I'm wiped out."

"No problem." Parneet flashed her a dazzling smile. "See you tomorrow? I should have some legal answers by then."

★★★

Daybreak filtered through the curtains. Dev pulled on her jeans without turning on the light. She didn't want her dad to see it shining under the door. Didn't want to talk to him yet. What would she say? "Let's go back to the way things were?" *No,* she thought fiercely, *there's no going back.* She yanked on her sweater and slipped into her boots.

Dev sneaked downstairs and wheeled her bicycle outside. She buckled her helmet, then pushed her bike to the street corner and swung on. In one fluid motion, she was across the empty intersection, winging through the cold Vancouver drizzle.

It was almost light by the time she reached the stable. She pulled open the end door and slipped her bike into the tack room. The warm barn smelled of hay and horses, and Dev was grateful to be the only person there. She pulled on her waterproof jacket and gloves, then went out through the back door.

Behind the barn, beside the ancient wagon wheel, stacked straw bales were covered by a blue tarp. Dev knew that Jerry kept old equipment back there, so she wedged herself behind the straw pile and searched around. *Aha!* she cheered as her foot hit an old-fashioned water trough. *I knew it!* She kicked the trough a couple of times until one end popped out from behind the tarp. Then she shimmied it free and dragged it into the clear.

The old enamel-and-metal trough had some sort of green slime growing on it. Dev rummaged around in the bathroom until she found a can of cleanser, then scrubbed the enamel until it shone. She fired up the hose and rinsed the trough carefully. Finally she dragged it into the barn and into Zim's stall.

"Sorry about this, Big Guy," Dev said cheerfully, "but the old automatic-water dish is going away." She reached up the pipe, found the valve, and cranked it off. The water dish hissed briefly, then fell silent.

Zim edged up to the trough and bumped it with his nose.

"That's right," Dev said, patting his neck affectionately. "That's your water dish now." She slipped back outside, then lugged in the hose and placed one end in the trough.

She didn't turn the water on. *Better wait for Elijah,* she thought, *or Zim might go ape.*

"What are you doing here so early?" Elijah's voice broke into her thoughts.

"Just the man I wanted to see."

"What's up?"

"We've got trouble," Dev said, shutting the stall door behind her. "I heard Ms. Caroline talking to Jerry and —"

Elijah cut her off. "I know all about that. She asked me, and I told her everything."

"Are we in a world of hurt?"

"Not really. She was mad at first, but then she said the truth probably would have come out sooner or later."

"Ms. Caroline said she's getting sued. Is that true?"

Elijah looked at the ground and kicked something imaginary. "Yeah, it is. She showed me the papers, Dev."

"What did they say?"

"A bunch of legal stuff. Basically they called Zim stolen property and said Ms. Caroline has thirty days to return him."

"A month?" Dev gasped. "No!"

"I'm so sorry."

"We'll fight it! My future uncle-in-law is a lawyer. He can help."

"Then he should definitely see those papers."

"I'd better talk to Ms. Caroline."

Elijah nodded. "Good luck with that. So what's with the hose?"

"I'm going to fill Zim's trough."

"Did we just time-travel back to 1912?"

"I'm giving him a crash course in fear management," Dev said grimly as she turned on the tap.

Zim plastered himself to the corner of his stall farthest from the trough.

"Shhh . . . settle down, Big Guy," Dev called soothingly.

Zim slowly moved to the trough again and snuffled around the edge. Then he backed away, snorting loudly.

"Zim! I know you're scared but it's just water." She leaned over and flicked some at him. "See?"

Zim shuddered the droplets off his coat, tossing his head.

"Look. Water." She bent and touched its rippled surface. Zim came closer.

"That's right." She lifted a handful of water and brought it to his lips. Zim's big pink tongue swept it away. Dev scooped another handful, but held it lower this time. Zim lowered his head to lick her hand. She did this five more times until his lips finally touched the water and he drank.

Dev trailed her hand across Zim's back as she stole away.

Ms. Caroline was in her office. Dev took a deep breath and knocked.

"Hello, Dev."

"Ms. Caroline, I am so sorry we made those phone calls. It was my fault, but I guess you already know that."

"Elijah told me it was his idea, although I had my suspicions."

"I realize we created a big mess, but there's a way to fix it. You know my uncle's getting married, right? His fiancée's brother is a lawyer. He said he would help us."

Ms. Caroline raised her eyebrows. "That's great, because we need all the help we can get. I have a copy of the legal papers here. If the lawyer would look at them, I'd appreciate it."

Dev took the papers and sat down. "I don't mean to be rude, Ms. Caroline, but Elijah and I wouldn't have been snooping if you had told me how you got Zim."

Ms. Caroline sighed. "You're right. I wish I'd made more effort to find out Zim's background. I didn't have many details. I just knew there was an incident and that a girl died."

"And that the girl's parents wanted to put Zim down?"

"Her father, mostly. Ron Miller. That's why the vet called me. He said he would give the horse to the SPCA if I'd adopt it from them. Since SPCA adoptions are confidential, he hoped the Millers wouldn't find out."

"Really?" Dev marvelled. "You honestly thought they'd never know?"

Ms. Caroline shrugged. "They told the vet they were moving, you know, to start over. And Zim's name used to be Shadow or something like that. So I thought . . . well . . . I don't know what I thought."

"I think you did the right thing."

"Then you're the only one."

Dev nodded as she left the office and went into the tack room. She put the papers in her backpack, then grabbed a coiled lead rope off its hook on the wall.

She walked into Zim's stall and clipped the rope to his halter. Zim's ears swivelled forward happily as he bobbed his head toward her. "I'm not going to let anything happen to you," she whispered fiercely. "That's a promise."

She led Zim into the hallway. He turned toward the indoor ring, but Dev gently pulled his head in the other direction. "Not today, Big Guy. We're going into the big wide world."

The barn door was open and the courtyard was wet. Rain was falling steadily. "Ready?" Dev asked when they reached the edge of the barn roof. Then she clicked her tongue twice, ordering Zim forward.

Zim moved into the courtyard with her, but his eyes had gone wide. He shivered off the raindrops but kept walking. Then, when they came to a huge puddle near the outdoor track, he stopped, pulling back.

"Quit it," Dev said in a warning tone. She didn't want to end up in the mud again. Zim stopped and lowered his head. Dev put her foot in the puddle and waited. To her surprise, Zim inched ahead and put one foot in the puddle, too.

"That's right," she said, moving forward a step. Zim matched her movement, placing his other front hoof in the water. "Good boy!" Dev patted his neck encouragingly.

They moved through the puddle step by step, side by side, until they came to the track. Then they ran around it until Dev finally had to stop, bent over and out of breath. "Okay, Big Guy," she gasped. "That's enough. Until you let me ride, we have to go at my pace."

They walked back through the puddle — again, step by step — and returned to the barn. Elijah was leaning on the doorpost, watching them.

"Not bad, eh?" Dev asked hopefully.

"Not bad when you're beside him," Elijah said, "but when are you going to try riding him?"

"Soon. Very soon."

Dev led Zim back to his stall, towelled him down and brushed him. She made sure he had lots of tender green timothy before leaving.

"Hey," Elijah called. "Your phone rang a bunch of times."

Dev went into the tack room to check her cell, which she'd left in her backpack. Her dad had phoned six times. She returned his call, hoping it would go straight to voice mail. But her dad answered the phone.

"Hi, it's me," Dev said. This was met with icy silence.

Followed by, "Get home — now!"

11 BACK IN THE SADDLE

Dev pushed her bike into the storeroom and rushed into the restaurant kitchen.

San looked up in surprise. "Hello, stranger!"

"Uncle San! Hi!" Dev said breathlessly. She hit the stairs and burst into the living room.

Dad was sitting at his desk, working on his laptop. "Hello," he mumbled without looking up.

Dev eased into a seat. "I know I should have told you I wanted to work with Zim. But I was afraid you might not let me. I'm sorry."

Dad sat back in his chair. He didn't seem angry anymore, just sad. "I've always depended on you, Dev. Maybe too much. Maybe that's the problem." He shrugged helplessly. "All I know is I'm losing you."

"You're not losing me, Dad. We just have different ideas about . . ." Dev's voice trailed off. *How do I finish that sentence? About what I should be doing? About my future? About who I am?*

"About what? My idea is that you belong here with your family."

"I know." *But I belong to South Hill, too,* she wanted to say, but couldn't. *With Elijah and Zim. Maybe even with Jenn and the other riders.*

"I want you to take over the restaurant someday."

Dev took a deep breath. "Dad, the restaurant is Ali's thing. He's always hanging around the kitchen helping San. You know he loves it."

"And you don't?"

"I didn't say that. I just want more."

Her father looked stunned. "Like what?"

Dev realized he probably couldn't imagine anything more. He and San had grown up working in their family's restaurant in Kerala. They didn't know anything else.

"I want to be a horse trainer, Dad. Equine Canada has a whole program that goes right from basic lessons all the way up to competition coaching. I already have most of the entrance qualifications." Dev didn't mention that she hoped to be on the Canadian Show Jumping Team someday, or that South Hill was facing a lawsuit. The first seemed next to impossible, and the second was all too real.

"Are your grades good enough?"

"They're getting there. I'm doing a lot better in school." Dev was relieved that it was actually true. "And I love training horses. It's a big responsibility, but it's worth it. When you understand how their minds work, you can see them growing and learning. They're so intelligent, it's breathtaking."

Dad's bewildered look was replaced by a smile of understanding. "Okay," he said, "we'll talk about this some more. It's a lot to think about, for both of us. Just remember there will always be a job here whenever you want one."

Dev smiled back. "I never thought I'd say this, but I do kind of miss working here."

"Okay, so you don't want to wash dishes anymore. But is there anything else around here that interests you?"

"I wouldn't mind learning how to deal with suppliers," Dev said. "Could I go with you to the warehouse sometimes?"

"Of course! You'll have to get up early, though."

"No problem," Dev said.

"Are you sure you're ready for the high-stakes world of wholesale buying? It's a thrill ride."

Dev laughed. "I'm ready, and I promise to help more with the wedding. I know there's a lot to do."

"I'm happy to hear that because Parneet will be here very soon. She needs help with clothes or something."

"I'll get ready."

"Thanks," Dad said, returning to his work. "I love you, you know."

"Love you, too."

By the time Dev had showered and dressed, Parneet

was in the living room, talking excitedly. Dev poked her head around the corner and called, "Hey Parneet! I'll be right there!"

Parneet excused herself and joined Dev in the hallway. "I have information," she whispered. They went into Dev's room and shut the door.

"They already served South Hill with legal papers," whispered Dev. "I brought copies."

"Good. Give them to me and I'll make sure my brother Raj sees them."

"Did he say anything? I mean, does he think we have a chance?"

"He needs to look into it. He doesn't think a judge will support the destruction of a horse for no reason, but there will likely be financial considerations."

"What do you mean?"

"Zim can probably be saved. but it could cost Ms. Caroline a lot of money. In fact, this could bankrupt South Hill Stables. That's why they need my brother's help." Parneet took the papers and put them in her purse. "Try not to worry too much. Raj is very good. He knows what to do."

"Thank you." Dev smiled feebly, but her mind was racing. *Try not to worry! If South Hill goes bankrupt, everything will be finished, Zim or no Zim.*

"Thank me by helping to find a wedding suit for your uncle. The one we ordered is not going to be here in time, so we have to start all over again."

"Okay, let's go."

Dev was surprised to find she enjoyed spending the rest of the day looking at wedding suits: cream ones with scarlet trim, black with gold accents, white with glimmering crystal beads. When they finally found the ideal one — the perfect size and the right colour to match Parneet's sari — it seemed like a miracle.

★★★

Dev arrived at the stable before anyone else, went into the tack room, and took down her saddle. It was dusty from lack of use, so she wiped it down with linseed oil, buffing the leather until it shone. Then she oiled the Glider's bridle and cleaned the snaffle bit with soap and hot water. She hung the bridle on a hook to let it dry.

Dev picked up her brush bucket and walked into Zim's stall, murmuring greetings. She cleaned him with the currycomb and smoothed his coat with the soft brush. Then she took her hoof pick and crouched beside his left foreleg. She tapped his knee gently, and Zim instantly raised his hoof and rested it in her hand. Dev ran the hoof pick around gently, clearing out bits of hay and manure. Then she moved to his hind foot.

Even though she knew Zim had been well trained, his willingness still amazed her sometimes. In a short time he had gone from being a wild thing — kicking and snorting in his stall or hiding timidly in the corner

— to a sweet, cooperative animal. She knew that Ms. Caroline had been right all along. Zim had potential. Boatloads of it.

After she was done grooming him, Dev snapped on the lead line and tied Zim to the hitching ring. She got her soft saddle pad and carried it into the stall.

"Now, we're going to put this on, and we're not going to freak out, okay?" she said. She moved close to Zim and slid the saddle pad onto his withers, right at the base of his neck. Then she slowly inched it into the correct position.

"Good boy. That's not so bad, is it?" She retrieved the saddle and slid it onto his back, as well. Zim bobbed his head a little and shivered.

"It's been a while, I know." Dev cinched the saddle. She slid her hand under the leather knot, checking its location behind his front leg and making sure it wouldn't rub or pinch.

"Excellent," she murmured, "if I do say so myself." She pulled down the stirrups and let them hang.

Then came the tricky part. She slid the bridle over her arm and returned to the stall, latching the door behind her. She didn't want any running away. She put the reins around Zim's neck and held them with her right hand. With her left, she unbuckled his halter and slipped it off.

Zim began to back away, but Dev corrected him, pulling sharply on the reins. "No, Zim. We're not finished yet."

Dev grasped the top of the bridle and held it firmly at Zim's forehead. Then, supporting the bit with her other hand, she slid it into his mouth, then up behind his back teeth. She slipped the bridle over his ears and buckled it under his chin. Finally she smoothed his forelock and stuck her fingers under the noseband to make sure it wasn't too tight.

The honey-coloured leather gleamed. Everything fit him perfectly.

Dev realized she'd broken out in a sweat, even though the whole process had gone smoothly and they'd reached another milestone. But there were many milestones yet to come.

Dev opened the door and walked Zim toward the indoor ring. She could hear Elijah whooping and hooting, urging on Jack. She watched them round the last barrel and sprint the length of the ring. "Best time ever!" Elijah shouted. "Way to go, Jack! Way to go!"

"Elijah," Dev called, "how long have you been here? I didn't even know you'd come in."

Elijah rode closer. "You were too busy prettying up the show jumper. Wow, you got him tacked up!"

Dev opened the gate, led Zim into the ring, and latched it again.

"Any news on that legal thing?" Elijah asked.

"Not yet, but we should know something soon."

"Are you going to take Zim for a run?"

Dev grinned. "I'm gonna try."

"Let me have one more crack at the barrels, okay?"

"No problem." Dev climbed the fence and perched on the top rail.

As Elijah positioned Jack at the start of the barrel-racing course, Zim's head went up. He seemed fascinated by Jack's every move.

Jack was hunkering down on his hindquarters, poised, ready to run. When Elijah urged him on, the stocky horse sprang. He leaped and raced for the first barrel.

Zim danced back, snorting. Clearly he wanted to go.

"You'll get your chance," Dev said. Then she had an idea. Zim's saddled back was right there, close beside her.

Without thinking about it, Dev laid her body across the saddle. Zim snorted again and skittered sideways.

Dev sat up and flipped her feet into the stirrups as Zim gave a few jumps forward. She slid her hands up the reins, instinctively looping them between her fingers, tightening them.

"Whoa," she said. "Wait for me, Big Guy."

By now Elijah and Jack had finished their race and were trotting around the ring. "C'mon," Elijah called, "let's put him through his paces."

Dev squeezed Zim's sides with both heels and he broke into a trot. She signalled again with one leg, and he flowed into an easy canter. When she laid the reins on his neck, Zim moved off the rail and cut across the middle of the ring. In the centre, Dev pressed her other leg to his side. It was the sign to change leads. Flinging his foreleg out effortlessly, Zim began to lead with his other foot. He made a smooth and graceful turn.

"This horse is fantastic!" Dev exclaimed. "Look at him! He's perfect!"

"Don't be too modest," Ms. Caroline called from the ringside. "The rider has something to do with it, too. You spent a lot of time getting him to this point."

"I want to try some jumps," Dev said breathlessly, pulling up. "Can I?"

"Can I stop you?"

"Nope."

Ms. Caroline came into the ring to hold Zim. "Watch it," she warned. "Not too high, you guys."

"We won't get crazy," Dev promised. She and Elijah ran around the ring, moving barrels out of the way and setting up jumps. They created a triple fence — each one higher than the one before — and Dev sped back to Zim.

"Start slowly," Ms. Caroline cautioned. "We don't know how he'll react." She boosted Dev onto Zim's back.

Dev popped her feet into the stirrup irons and hunched forward, pressing her legs into the padded knee rolls. She gathered the reins. They rested firmly between the pinkie and ring finger of each hand, looping between each index finger and thumb. Now she was in complete control.

She leaned forward and spoke to Zim softly. "We're going to jump now, Big Guy. Wait for me. I'll tell you when to go."

Zim swivelled his ears back and tossed his head.

Dev pressed her heel to his side and Zim broke into a canter. They loped smoothly once around the ring, then moved off the rail and toward the jumps. Dev leaned forward slightly and Zim picked up speed. When they reached the first jump, she lowered the reins so they were far forward beside his neck. She pressed with both heels and Zim sprang, front feet together. Dev felt him surge up, higher than he needed to go, powerful as a coiled spring released. Zim landed, gathered his hindquarters, and jumped — confidently, easily — again and again.

The sound of his feet thumping onto the earth was beautiful.

12 DARK HORSE

When Dev and Zim finally came to a stop, it was to the sound of applause. Did Dev recognize the cheering voice? She shaded her eyes, peering into the dim bleachers. "Dad!?"

Her father walked down the stairs, still clapping.

"Mr. Rani!" Ms. Caroline exclaimed. "It's lovely to see you after all this time."

Dev balanced in one stirrup and sprang off. "Dad, what are you doing here?"

"Hello to you, too," her father said. "Actually, I came to talk to Ms. Caroline Brennan about your future. And Parneet said something about a legal action. I want to know what's happening and maybe help, if I can."

Ms. Caroline nodded. "Come into my office. Parneet kindly arranged some help for me, and the lawyer has already been in touch. He's working on a countersuit and we can file . . ." Ms. Caroline's voice trailed off as they went into the office and shut the door.

Elijah smiled encouragingly. "It'll be all right."

Dev wasn't so sure. She shrugged and walked Zim back to his stall. As she was grooming him and then getting him an extra-large ration of pellets, she tried to hear what Ms. Caroline was saying. But only the occasional word came through.

Dev washed up and changed, then waited anxiously in the hall.

Finally the door opened and Dad walked out. Dev couldn't quite gauge his expression. "Come on," he said. "I'll give you a lift home."

"Bye, Ms. Caroline," Dev said dispiritedly as she rolled her bike outside.

Dad put his arm around her awkwardly. "Don't look so upset," he said. "It'll be okay."

Dev loaded her bike into the back of the van and climbed into the passenger seat.

Dad started to put the key in the ignition, then stopped. He sat back and looked at her. "You know, I considered pulling you out of riding because I'm worried you'll get your heart broken."

"Dad, no . . ."

"Let me finish. But when I saw you and Zim jumping like that, I couldn't believe it. You are so good! You make it look easy!"

"It's not easy."

"I know that." Dad started the car and pulled onto South Hill's long driveway. "I saw the look on Ms. Brennan's face and your friend Elijah's smile. They are proud of you! They're, I don't know, in awe of you. What you can do is special."

Dev smudged a tear away with her sleeve. Dad had never said anything like that before. Not ever.

"I told Ms. Brennan I want to sponsor you. And I promise to help you fight for that horse, as well."

Dev found his words mind-boggling.

"Ms. Brennan told me something else, too, but I'm not supposed to say anything."

"What?"

"Don't worry. It's good."

"Dad! You can't just say that and not tell me."

"Oh look," he said, "we're home now."

"Dad," Dev said in her most menacing tone.

Her father grinned impishly as he parked the van, grabbed the keys, and hopped out. "Too much to do. Got to run."

Dev pulled out her bike, shaking her head. *It's official,* she thought. *Everybody around me is totally nuts.*

Parneet was in the restaurant kitchen, showing San and Ali a blueprint of the reception's seating arrangement.

Leave it to an engineer to make a detailed drawing for sixty guests! Dev couldn't help it; she laughed as she walked upstairs.

★★★

The next day was Monday again. But Monday wasn't a day to dread anymore, now that she didn't have to rush from the stables to the restaurant to wash dishes and help close up. Even school wasn't so bad. It was a lot easier now that Parneet was tutoring her. A lot easier now that she was prepared.

She couldn't wait to get to the stables after school. When she got there, she dumped her bike in the tack room and knocked on Ms. Caroline's office door.

"Come in," Ms. Caroline said, and gestured toward the chair across from her. "I'm glad you're here. There are a few things we need to discuss."

Dev sat down. "Oh, yeah?" she asked, trying to sound casual.

"Jerry has decided to retire. He'll still be around — and involved with South Hill — but he doesn't want to give lessons anymore."

"Oh."

"You said you were interested in teaching, so I think you should enroll in Equine Canada's coaching program. Your father has already agreed to pay your fees."

"My dad?" So that was what he meant by sponsoring her!

"He's going to cover your show entrance costs, too. We'll have to work hard next season if we want scouts from Jump Canada to notice you."

"That's awesome!" *But also a lot of money,* Dev worried.

"In the meantime, you've definitely been noticed around here. Several of Jerry's students asked if you could give them riding lessons once he retires."

Dev's mind spun. This was her chance to help out with the cost of training and competing! But she couldn't imagine any of the other riders taking instruction from her. "You think they'll actually listen to me?"

"They'll have to!" Ms. Caroline laughed. "You'll be the teacher!"

"Really?"

"Really. You're not quite old enough, but we can get started. You're already a Level 6 rider, so you just need courses in equestrian theory. Then you have to log mentoring hours, kind of like an apprenticeship. I can help you with that."

"How do I sign up?"

"I've got the papers right here."

Dev took the papers and quickly glanced through information about levels and testing and program certificates. She signed.

"You'll be glad to know I've hired a new groom." Ms. Caroline grinned. "I know you'll miss the manure, but you won't have time for anything except teaching and riding."

"I can't thank you enough!"

"Oh," Ms. Caroline said, "I almost forgot the best part. I've decided to keep Mirror Glider here. She can be your lesson horse, in case some of your students don't have their own."

"*Yes!*"

"And we're going to have to start looking for a new show jumper for you."

"A new jumper? What about Zim?"

"I promise we'll do our best, but we may not be able to keep him. You need to think about —"

"No," Dev said firmly. "I want Zim. Only Zim."

"Oh, Dev, I owe you an apology. I made a bad decision bringing him here."

"No, you didn't. You were totally right about him. He's got so much potential! And he's not dangerous. I'll prove it."

"That's not the point. The reality is, I don't own Zim, and if Ron Miller has his way, I never will."

"Mr. Miller can still change his mind —"

"Dev," Ms. Caroline said.

"Just listen! We need to show Mr. Miller how well his daughter trained Zim. That horse is Janine's legacy — Zim is all that's left of her! How could the Millers want to destroy that?"

"I don't know. Look, Raj pushed back the handover date to ninety days but after that —"

"Then I have ninety days to convince Mr. Miller."

"Convince him of what?"

"That Zim is a good horse! That he won't ever hurt anybody!" *And that he belongs here, with me.*

13 NATURAL-BORN JUMPER

Dev brought Zim to the indoor ring for the fourth time in a week. Every day that week she had added more jumps. In addition to the triple fences, there were two double rails, three high singles, and a castle jump. The water hazard was next.

She and Elijah rigged up a water jump using an old plastic sled and a bunch of sawdust. It was a smaller jump than any in a competition, but still a water jump. Elijah named it the not-so-hazardous water hazard.

Today's the day, Dev thought. She put her foot into the stirrup, stood briefly, then eased into the saddle. She moved Zim to the rail and signalled him to trot. He began instantly, then sped to his dazzling float. Dev timed her posting to the uncanny pause — the moment the world seemed to stop — that happened every time Zim threw out a front foot. They circled the ring three times, then started to canter.

Dev leaned low, perched on Zim's withers. They raced toward the triple fences, which were much higher now. They had done this so often, Dev barely needed to signal anymore. All she had to do was balance and drop her hands, and Zim would leap.

She could feel the front of Zim's body lift high as he curled his forelegs together. Then the power shifted to his hindquarters as his back legs bent, straightened, lifted. He tucked them close to his stomach and was, for a second, airborne. So was Dev. At the top of the jump, she was off the saddle, suspended above him. Her hands, still holding the reins, rested perfectly on his mane.

Then the moment was past and they were on their way down. The power moved to Zim's shoulders as he straightened his front legs, getting ready to land. His hooves hit the ground, flipping back as his body moved forward. His back feet landed just after his front ones.

There was time for only one step before he had to jump again, sailing smoothly over the second fence. Dev tightened her legs, gripping the saddle's knee roll, and leaned far forward. Her hands followed Zim's head, giving him enough rein to stretch but still staying in contact. It was the only way they could communicate now that they were mid-jump.

They thumped to the ground again. Flew again. The third fence surprised Zim a little and he had to correct himself and go higher. Dev winced, afraid to hear the sound of a hoof hitting a rail. She didn't.

They cleared the jump and Dev sat straighter, looking toward the next hurdle. They moved across the ring easily and over the castle. Then they took the highest single rail and, at the far end of the course, changed direction.

Now the water jump, Dev thought. She steered Zim toward it and pulled gently on both reins to slow him down. As they cantered toward the water, Zim let out a warning snort.

Dev clamped her legs around him and said loudly, "Let's go, Zim."

When they reached the hazard, Zim veered to the right and ran around it. Dev slid toward his left shoulder but recovered.

"Ah-ah," she said firmly. "Quit it."

She circled the ring again and directed Zim to the water, clenching her legs, ready for anything.

This time, Zim spun and stopped. Dev found herself hanging from his neck, upside down. "Let's try that again, shall we?" she asked grimly, lowering herself to the ground.

She got back on and patted Zim encouragingly. "You can do this, Big Guy," she said. "You don't have to get your feet wet. Jump over it."

They cantered around the ring again and came directly at the water hazard. Zim stopped dead. Dev flew right over his head. She landed in the water, flat on her back.

Zim tried to run away, but Dev was still holding the reins, her arm extended.

"Very funny," she said. She got up and brushed herself off, although it was pretty pointless. Her jodhpurs were completely soaked. She pulled Zim toward her, hand over hand. "See? Everything is fine. Just. Jump. Over. It." She did a little hop over the water hazard. "See?"

"Okay, let's try something different." Stationing herself at his left shoulder, Dev took a deep breath. Then she ran beside him around the ring, barely keeping up with his extended trot. As they came toward the water hazard, Dev yelled, "Up!"

And Zim jumped.

She ran with him a few more paces, then pulled up. "Good boy," she said, patting Zim enthusiastically. "Yes, you're such a good boy." Then she ran him around the ring again, and he jumped again on her verbal command. They did this six more times.

Dev crouched and put her hands on her knees, breathing hard. "All this running is why you have to be in good shape to ride a jumper," she gasped. "Okay, Big Guy, playtime is over. Let's try doing it my way."

She got back on Zim and took him around the ring in a steady trot. As they approached the water jump, she hunkered down, clinging as tightly as she knew how. When they reached the hazard, Dev leaned forward and said, "Up!"

It was the magic word.

They flew over the water hazard, then turned and

jumped the last two single rails. "That's right," Dev said, patting him. "You got it!"

She took him to their starting position and began again, around the ring, over the triple fences, the castle, and the high single rail. When they ran at the water hazard, Dev said, "Up!" — and they soared. Zim took the last two rails without breaking stride.

Dev had never been so happy in her whole life. She sprang off and threw her arms around Zim, hugging him like she never wanted to let go.

Dev walked Zim into his stall, took off the saddle, and placed it in the corner. Then she unbuckled his bridle and gently slid the bit out of his mouth. She put on his halter and tied him to the hitching ring. "Although," she said, thumping his shoulder affection-ately, "there's really no point tying you up. I don't think there's a knot known to man you can't undo!"

She carried her saddle to the tack room, almost bumping into Jenn.

"Hey, Dev," Jenn said. "Can I ask you something?"

"Sure. Come talk to me while I take care of Zim." Dev grabbed her brushes.

Sure enough, Zim had untied the knot and the rope was dangling free. But this time, he didn't run. He turned his head toward her and nickered. Dev could have sworn he was laughing.

Jenn followed her into the stall. "I was wondering... did Ms. Caroline talk to you yet?"

"About?"

"I asked her to ask you . . . um, if you might want to give me riding lessons. Heather and Carrie asked, too."

Dev didn't quite know what to say.

"She'd love to!" Elijah hollered from the hallway.

"Yeah. Yes!" Dev said, recovering. "I'm honoured that you would ask me. Ms. Caroline will need to be there, of course. I have to log, like, a hundred mentoring hours before I can teach on my own. But thank you! That's great!"

"I'm not supposed to tell you, but even Anna wants your help," Jenn said softly, "to get Fire Dancer over his fear of the castle jump."

"I'd be happy to help her," Dev said. "All she has to do is ask."

"And pay!" Elijah yelled.

Dev and Jenn cracked up.

"Well, you're busy," Jenn said, grinning. "I'd better go."

After she left, Dev couldn't stop smiling. She brushed Zim down, head to tail, then buckled on his green stable blanket. She fed Zim and gave him fresh water before helping Elijah take care of the other horses.

"Do you want me to look after Zim tomorrow?" Elijah asked, pulling apart a hay bale.

"Wait. What?"

"Aren't you supposed to be getting all bridesmaidy?"

The wedding was the next day. Dev had almost

forgotten. "Oh, right," she said, smacking her forehead. "I was hoping to make it to the barn, but I guess that's not going to happen."

"It doesn't matter," Elijah said dramatically. "The world is coming to an end, anyway. I mean, you wearing a dress?"

Dev punched him on the arm.

"See how ladylike you've become already?"

Dev shook her head and laughed. "Thanks, Elijah. Yes, please look after him for me."

"How many favours do you owe me now?"

"An infinite number. I can't possibly count."

The stars were beginning to have a hard wintry glint. By the time Dev got home, the restaurant was closed. She gazed up at a huge neon sign that said *Kerala* in curvy red letters. It was new; the old sign had looked like something from a 1950s diner. A notice on the door read: Closed for Private Function. Underneath, a separate one announced, Dev guessed, the same thing in Malayalam.

She wheeled her bike into a flurry of activity. Dad and San were loading up the industrial refrigerator with prepared food. Manu and Parneet were inside the restaurant, fluffing tablecloths and placing centrepieces. Ali was everywhere Manu was, trying to help.

"Dad!" Dev called. "What can I do?"

"Could you wash the floor?"

"No problem! I'll get changed and be right back."

"What happened to you?" Dad put his hands on Dev's shoulders and spun her around.

"Just a little water-related issue," Dev said. "No big deal."

Dad gave her a stern look.

"The important thing is," Dev went on, "I figured it out. Zim jumps over water now!" Dev danced happily up the stairs.

They spent the rest of the evening washing and polishing, placing and replacing, until everything gleamed.

"It's gorgeous, Parneet," Dev said, pushing the hair out of her eyes. "Everything is perfect."

"We owe it all to you and Manu." Parneet smiled.

"Mostly Manu," Ali piped up.

"He's one of my peeps," Dev said, bowing, "so I don't mind taking the credit. You're welcome."

14 VICTORY LAP

Dev walked Zim around the outdoor track to warm him up for the jump course. "Going last will be hard, Big Guy," she warned him. "You have to be patient and listen to me, just like we practiced." She heard Jerry's voice announcing that the jumping competition would soon begin in the indoor ring.

It was an exhibition show, not a true competition. *And really,* Dev thought, *it's a retirement party for Jerry. A strange retirement party, but then, this is South Hill we're talking about.*

Her mind bounced back to San's wedding. It was a crazy blur. The salon, getting manicures and matching makeup with Parneet and her sisters. The ceremony, in a church full of pale green roses almost exactly the shade of Parneet's sari. The restaurant, full of flame-coloured maple leaves and golden oak. And then photographs, speeches, food, and more food.

She remembered what Raj had said to her after the ceremony. She knew he'd meant well, but his attempt to be comforting had the opposite effect. "Zim can be saved," he'd said, "but only if he leaves South Hill."

Either way, Dev would lose him.

She walked Zim to the back gate so they could watch the other jumpers. Her future students. Strange but true.

Ms. Caroline walked toward her, smiling. "I don't know if you can see it from here, but I have a surprise for you." She gestured at the indoor ring.

Dev moved closer and strained her eyes, willing them to adjust to the indoor light after the bright sunshine. "What the...?" she sputtered. "How did you...?" There was a water jump. A real one.

"Elijah did it —" Ms. Caroline beamed "— with a tarp and a lot of elbow grease. It's exactly to the Hunter-Jumper Association's specifications."

"That's great," Dev said. "But, um, are you sure a new water jump is the best idea right now?"

"It doesn't matter," Ms. Caroline said firmly. "This is just for fun. If Zim shies, he shies. You'll have plenty of time to get him used it."

Easy for you to say, Dev thought. *You're not the one who'll end up on her butt in front of everybody's parents.* "Okay," she said, "you know I love a challenge."

Dev watched the first riders move through the course. They weren't bad, she mused, but they definitely needed work. She was already thinking of posture exercises to give them, and of other things she wanted to teach them.

"And now, ladies and gentlemen," Jerry thundered, "we request your patience as we adjust the jumps for our next team."

Elijah and Ms. Caroline ran onto the course. They raised all the triple fences, then cranked up the height of the single rails. They looked over to Dev while they were working and, every time, Dev jutted up her thumb to say, "Higher." At last, everything was ready.

Ms. Caroline opened the gate as Jerry announced, "We're proud to introduce, in his debut performance, our newest jumper — Zim!" Then, as an afterthought, he added, "Along with our own Dev Rani." Laughter rippled through the crowd.

Dev smiled briefly, then focused all her energy on Zim. If she wanted to give him time to check out the water hazard, they'd have to take a long run at the high fence. Firmly gathering the reins, Dev moved Zim onto the rail and signalled. He broke into a slow canter and circled the course.

At the far side of the ring, Dev pulled Zim off the rail and changed direction. She clamped her heels to his sides, telling him to run. He sped up to a near gallop and sailed over the castle jump. Then they turned sharply, speeding past the water hazard, and cleared the highest single rail.

The crowd gasped. Actually gasped.

Zim's jumping form was perfect: front feet curled, hindquarters high, back feet raised, then tucked — with only a split second to spare — as his front feet hit the ground. As they circled the end of the ring, Dev leaned over and patted him, murmuring praise. Then she hunkered down, gripping the knee roll tightly, as Zim ran toward the water jump.

It seemed huge — far bigger than anything even she and the Glider had attempted — and there were little trees on either side of it. Dev heard Zim's hooves beat and beat as they drew closer. She moved her hands forward, leaning far up his neck, and cried, "Up!"

Zim jumped up — much higher than he needed to — stretching his legs full out. As they hit the ground and turned toward the triple fences, Dev felt sweat drip down her face. They cleared the remaining hurdles one by one.

The onlookers went wild as Dev slowed Zim and let him circle the course one last time. When they finally stopped, she felt weak in the knees. She could only imagine how Zim felt. She put her arms around his neck and dismounted, showboat-style, to bow to the crowd.

Zim extended one foreleg, curled the other beneath him, and bowed, too.

Dev shook her head in amazement. *Another thing Janine must have taught him!* "Come on, you ham," she grinned.

Everyone was still laughing and clapping as Dev led Zim out of the ring. She saw a man approach Ms. Caroline, and she turned to him, her face friendly and open.

That couldn't be the scout from Jump Canada, could it? Dev wondered as she and Zim drew closer to them. She couldn't make out what Ms. Caroline was saying, but now she looked upset.

Dad jumped down from the bleachers to join Ms. Caroline. "Mr. Miller, please," Dev heard him say, "if it's a matter of buying the horse, I'm more than willing to do that."

Dev stopped dead. This wasn't a guy from Jump Canada or any kind of scout. It was Janine Miller's father.

She went cold. She wanted to run away, but where would they go? She knew that she had to face this and that she'd only have one shot at it.

Dev walked right up to them, pretending she hadn't noticed they were arguing. "Did you *see* that?" she broke in. "Wasn't Zim awesome? He's such a good horse, so well trained. Somebody really made an investment in him."

The three adults all stared at her.

Dev smiled innocently. "Could you believe it? A regulation water jump — one he'd never seen before — and he went straight over it."

"Dev," Ms. Caroline said, "would you excuse us, please? We're in the middle of something here."

"No," Dev answered, squaring her shoulders. "I think you need to excuse *us*. Mr. Miller, may I have a word?"

Ms. Caroline looked shocked, her father astonished. His mouth actually hung open for a second before he recovered and moved politely away. Ms. Caroline followed him almost meekly.

"Dev Rani, I presume," Mr. Miller said.

"I'm pleased to meet you, sir," Dev said. "Honestly."

"I suppose you know why I'm here."

"I do. I know everything, and I'm so sorry for your loss."

"You can't possibly understand —"

"I understand more than you think I do, Mr. Miller," Dev cut in. "Like, I understand how hard your daughter worked to train this horse. She really loved him, didn't she."

Mr. Miller looked like he might cry. Zim moved forward and lowered his head.

"He wants you to pet him," Dev said. "Do you want to?"

"Yeah, I do," Mr. Miller said. He slid his hand down Zim's neck and patted the horse's firm shoulder. "I miss you, Big Guy."

"That's what I call him, too!" Dev stroked Zim's mane. They stood in silence, focusing on the horse. Then Dev asked, very quietly, "Do you really think she would want him to die?"

Mr. Miller continued to stroke Zim's neck. An eon passed. "No, I sure don't," he said at last.

Dev felt faint.

"You'd better get your father over here," Mr. Miller said. "There are a few things we need to straighten out."

Dev waved to her dad and Ms. Caroline, beckoning them over.

"I want you to know this is not about money," Mr. Miller said to Dad. "I don't care about that. I just don't want anyone else to get hurt. I can't be held responsible."

"I'll take responsibility," Dad said.

"I won't get hurt," Dev said at the same instant.

"See that you don't," Mr. Miller ordered, looking into Dev's eyes. "I mean it." He turned to Dad and Ms. Caroline. "And nobody rides this horse but Dev Rani, is that understood?"

Dev watched her dad and Janine's dad shake on the deal.

"There's one last thing," Dad said. "Please drop the lawsuit."

"It's done," Mr. Miller said. "We're square. Oh, except I should give you his pedigree papers. Have your lawyer draw up a transfer of ownership document and I'll sign it."

"Thank you!" Dev cried. "Thank you! Thank you!" The words weren't enough. No words would ever be enough.

"Looks like you've got a new horse —" Ms. Caroline smiled "— but you'd better be planning to keep him at South Hill!"

"You know it," Dev said, "I would never . . ." She became aware that someone was calling her name.

It was Jerry, hollering into the bullhorn, "Dev Rani, return to the ring for your second circuit before we have to adjust all these jumps again!"

"C'mon," Elijah urged as he pulled the gate open, "your future is waiting."

With a last grateful smile at Mr. Miller, Dev turned and led Zim into the ring. Everything seemed sharper somehow, brighter than before, as she swung into the saddle. At Jerry's signal, she moved Zim to the rail and began.

The future no longer felt like a ticking bomb. The future was this horse, her new job, the next show season, and . . . who knew? Maybe even a new team.

They moved smoothly into a canter, and with each step, the past dropped away. Not Janine, though. She would stay with them always. But the fear and sadness faded with every fence they took.

As they sailed over the castle, Dev pictured herself in muddy coveralls, pitching straw, then lugging bus pans, loading a steaming dishwasher, so afraid that her time as a rider might suddenly just end. She shook her head to sweep it all away. She leaned ahead, perfectly balanced on her stirrups, and tightened her hold on the reins.

They were ready to fly.

They turned to the water hazard. The ground flowed beneath them. Dev flicked her hands forward and time stopped. Zim jumped, soaring higher and higher. He leaped straight over the hazard — fearlessly, with a kind of wild joy — and left it in the dust.

BE A
PRO! KNOW THE LINGO.

APPALOOSA: A North American breed of horse with a distinctive coat of dark spots on a light background.

ARABIAN HORSE: One of the oldest breeds in the world, relatively small with a delicate head, flowing mane, and a tail that arches during a gallop.

BARREL RACING: A Western riding event that involves a race around three barrels set up in a triangle pattern.

BAY: A dark brown horse with a black mane and tail.

BIT: The metal mouthpiece of a horse's bridle.

BRIDLE: The leather headgear of a horse, made up of a headstall, bit, and reins.

CANTER: A horse's slow gallop.

CASTLE JUMP: A large jump made of Styrofoam blocks.

CREW / RING CREW: People who set up jumps, change the height of jumps, and repair jumps that have been knocked down.

CURRYCOMB: A stiff horse brush.

ENGLISH RIDING: Horse-riding with English-style gear, used in such formal events as hunting and jumping.

ENGLISH SADDLE: A light saddle used in English riding.

FERRIER: A person who shoes horses.

FLAKE: A slice of a bale of hay that is fed to a horse, usually weighing about 1 ½ kilograms (3 pounds).

FORELOCK: The lock of hair over a horse's forehead.

GAIT: The way a horse moves forward — walking, trotting, cantering, or galloping.

GALLOP: A horse's fastest pace.

GIRTH: A leather or cloth band fastened under the stomach of a horse to keep the saddle in place.

GYMKHANA: A fast-paced horse-riding competition featuring Western events and games.

HALTER: Rope or cloth headgear for horses with a metal ring to which a lead rope can be attached, and no bit or reins.

HEADSTALL: The part of a bridle or halter that fits around a horse's head.

HITCHING RING: A large metal ring on the wall of a horse's stall to which a lead rope can be attached.

HOCK: The lower joint of a horse's hind leg.

HOOF PICK: A small metal hook used to remove stones and dirt from a horse's hoof.

HORSESHOE: A U-shaped piece of metal nailed to the bottom of a horse's hoof to protect it.

JUMP: An obstacle, usually made of wood, to be jumped by a horse.

KNEE ROLL: padding at the front of an English saddle where a rider's knee rests.

LEAD: The foot a horse extends first while cantering; when a cantering horse changes direction, it must first change its lead.

LEAD ROPE: A rope with a metal clip on one end that can be attached to a horse's halter.

LEVEL 6: Equine Canada's 10-level English rider program measures a rider's level of achievement. A Level 6 rider is able to take a horse through its paces rhythmically and evenly, and can jump a fence at least 2 ft., 6 in. (0.8 m) high.

LUNGE LINE: A long rope a horse trainer uses to make a horse canter in a circle.

NOSEBAND / NOSE STRAP: The part of a bridle or halter that fits over a horse's nose.

POSTING: An English-style rider's up-and-down action in the saddle that works with the rhythm of the horse's gait; posting makes the rider more comfortable and protects the horse's back.

QUARTERHORSE: A stocky breed of horse that can run a quarter mile faster than any other breed and is ideal for herding cattle.

RAIL: A horizontal wooden bar on a jump or fence.

REIN: A long narrow strap attached to a bit and used to guide a horse.

RING: A fenced-in area used for exercising, training, and showing horses, sometimes rectangular in shape.

SNAFFLE BIT: A gentle bit that is jointed in the middle.

TACK: Saddles, bridles, and other gear for horses.

TACK ROOM: The room in a stable where tack is kept.

THOROUGHBRED: A tall English breed of horse used for racing, as well as fox hunting and jumping.

TIMOTHY HAY: A common hay made from dried timothy grass.

TRAIL CLASS: A Western riding competition that test horse's strength and obedience.

TROT: A steady pace faster than a walk and slower tha a canter.

VERTICAL: A very high jump with a single rail.

WATER JUMP / WATER HAZARD: A wide jump over water

WESTERN RIDING: Horse-riding with Western gear, based on skills used to herd domestic animals on ranches or farms.

WESTERN SADDLE: A heavy saddle with a high back designed for comfort during long hours on horseback.

WITHERS: The area at the top of a horse's shoulders between its neck and back.